SCHOOL DAZE

Dedicated to Jade

We would like to thank Sam Lewis and Savi Hensman for their voluntary help in producing this book.

First published in 1990 by Sheba Feminist Publishers, 10A Bradbury Street, London N16 8JN.

Cover and book design: Spark Ceresa
Typeset by Russell Press, Nottingham, England
Printed and bound by Cox and Wyman, Reading, England

British Library Cataloguing and Publication Data available

SCHOOL DAZE

Stories edited by Christina Dunhill
and Michelle McKenzie

 Sheba Feminist Publishers

CONTENTS

C O N T E N T S

INTRODUCTION

Welcome to School Daze! An exciting new collection of modern day stories for fast living girls and boys, from eleven new writers to be reckoned with.

Upbeat and filled with bursts of energy, these true to life stories pull no punches. Whether funny, fantastical or sad, they will bring you face to face with real life drama in the classroom, the home and the playground. Challenging, provoking, scary, witty and sometimes hilarious, there's something in School Daze for everyone.

Can classroom rivals, Jasmine and leader of the girls' gang, Tossie Thompson ever stop fighting?

How many tall stories can you really tell and get away with? Lima finds she's told one too many.

What would you do if you thought your teacher was from Mars! Can Evelyn and her friends outwit the alien?

There's only one way to find out!!..........
We hope you enjoy it.

Christina Dunhill & Michelle McKenzie.

THE INVASION OF THE HISTORY TEACHER

BARBARA BENNETT

On Monday evening, after homework and trumpet practice, Evelyn and Junior Henry sat like good children, side by side on the settee, their hands folded neatly in their laps.

They remained perfectly meek and still as Mr Henry put on his work clothes and left for his night shift. But at the sound of the front door closing behind him they sprang up, laughing, shouting, singing and fighting, just like a cork exploding out of a bottle of fizzy drink.

After a while their mother, who was tired, announced it was time for bed. As usual Evelyn and Junior did not agree.

'M-u-u-m! It's not dark yet and Daddy said we could stay up to watch the scary film on telly tonight.'

Mrs Henry shook her head in disbelief.

'He did, Mum, really. Junior, tell Mum, didn't Dad say we could stay up for the film?' Evelyn prompted.

But Junior was a very straightforward boy.

'Nope,' he said, and began to howl very noisily at the face Evelyn pulled, which Mrs Henry explained was because he was tired and should be in bed.

A short time later found them tucked up in the back bedroom with the light switched off. But though they were down, they were not defeated. Their tightly closed eyes and the low rumbling snores, loud enough to be heard through the bedroom door, were just for show.

Evelyn had invented The Method-of-staying-awake-however-tired-you-are especially for occasions such as this. An uncomfortable but effective system, it consisted of sticking the right leg, the one furthest from the wall, as far out of the bedclothes as was physically possible without falling out of bed. It made her leg hurt and it made Junior laugh till tears came to his eyes, but there are drawbacks with any original idea! It was clean, it was noiseless, if you ignored Junior's snickering, and it almost always worked; three distinct advantages over Evelyn's alarm clock.

Slowly the minutes ticked by. The sounds of Mrs Henry pottering about the flat gradually subsided, and the sounds of Junior's snoring became more and more convincing. At last, Evelyn decided it would be safe to get up. Junior was woken with a shrewdly judged pinch. It was sharp, but not quite sharp enough to make him yell out loud.

They tip-toed gingerly down the passage to the living room. Their weary mother, as expected, was sound asleep in front of the flickering television screen. Junior stood on the threshold for some moments, staring in awe and fascination at his slumbering parent, before plucking up the courage to snatch a cushion and dart to safety behind the settee. Meanwhile, Evelyn rummaged under Mrs Henry's knitting for the remote control. She carefully found the right channel, set the volume low and then retired behind the settee to enjoy the evening's scary science fiction feature film, with her trembling younger brother.

Next morning at school, Evelyn attempted to impress her friend with an account of the film.

'What a shame you missed it! You'd have been scared stiff. My little brother got so scared when the monster from outer space invaded, he...'

'When the what did what?' interrupted Serena irritably. Possibly her least favourite pastime was hearing Evelyn's accounts of films she had missed.

'When the monster plants invaded — tried to take

over...' Evelyn lowered her voice to a spine chilling whisper, '...and they took over people's bodies.'

'Whatever for?' asked Serena, sounding not the faintest bit interested.

'So no one would know they were invading, and so they'd get around quicker I expect,' Evelyn explained.

'Plants aren't scary, who cares if they invade.'

Evelyn sighed at her friend's insensitive attitude.

'These plants don't stand around looking pretty in pots! These plants wait till you fall asleep and then grow a great big alien pod next to you that copies your body. When it's finished, out pops a new you, and your own mother wouldn't know the difference!'

Serena's imagination was stirred.

'N-a-a-a-sty...' she murmured, 'so, you might think you were talking to your best friend and really all the time it's a monster plant that only looks like her!'

'Ugh!' said Evelyn, suddenly uneasy.

Serena reached under her desk, detached a lump of chewing gum and popped it into her mouth, from whence it re-emerged seconds later as a large pink bubble. Slowly it swelled and then burst.

'Ugh!' repeated Evelyn, shuddering. Sometimes she would almost prefer a monster plant from Mars, she thought.

Evelyn yawned, carefully shielding her open mouth with a history book.

'Right boys and girls, I want you all to turn to page sixteen in your book of Great Discoveries,' said Mrs Warren, class Two B's history teacher, '...and make notes on the section about Christopher Columbus landing on the islands later to be known as the West Indies.'

Although Evelyn would never admit it, she was tired after her late night. Without thinking, she extended her right leg up and out from her desk. The Method-of-staying-awake-however-tired-you-are had become quite automatic.

'Ahem!...You there with the leg. In my classes, it is enough to raise your hand when you want to ask a question,' called

Mrs Warren. Evelyn's yawn froze into a gape of horror. Suddenly she was wide awake, another success for The Method!

'Well, what is it? What did you want to ask?' inquired the relentless Mrs Warren.

Evelyn thought quickly.

'Er...Um...Er, I was thinking, our history book should really be called Great Invasions. I mean it can't have been much of a discovery, Columbus finding the West Indies, when there were people already living there. They must have noticed it, surely?'

'Get on with your work and stop quibbling,' snapped Mrs Warren.

Evelyn lowered her leg and returned to studying her textbook but before long, the urge to yawn returned. Cautiously, Evelyn looked around. Mrs Warren was standing by the window, blinking out at the sunlight. She appeared to be completely absorbed, despite a view empty of all but clouds, sky, and the tops of buildings.

'She looks strange today, doesn't she?' commented Serena at the next desk.

'Yeah,' Evelyn agreed, 'sort of blank and different, like there was something missing.'

'And why is she standing at the window, batting and blinking her eyelids in that weird way?'

Evelyn thought about this.

'Perhaps she's fallen in love with the window cleaner!'

Serena shook her head and, leaning forward, beckoned Evelyn to move a little closer.

'Suppose...' she hissed, 'just suppose she's signalling to Martian spaceships in Morse code, telling them when to invade!'

Whether it was due to Serena's penetrating whisper, or whether she had been alerted by more alien means, Mrs Warren chose that very moment to bring an end to their discussion.

'Don't think that I don't know you two are wasting my lesson gossiping, Evelyn Henry and Serena Adebola. I've got eyes in the back of my head! Now, get on, or I shall keep you both behind for detention.'

'I bet she really has got eyes in the back of her head,' murmured Evelyn as they began making notes.

An hour later, a small excited group clustered around Evelyn and Serena in the school playground.

'Let's get this straight,' said Ellen, who was not entirely convinced. 'You say our history teacher is a vegetable from Mars, invading the Earth disguised as Mrs Warren?'

'It's obvious,' said Serena simply.

'We all saw her signal to alien spaceships through the classroom window, didn't we?' added Evelyn.

'Maybe, maybe not,' said Rowan, who shared Ellen's doubts.

'Well, anyone can see there's something different about her today.'

Several heads nodded in agreement with this.

'And she even said herself that she had eyes in the back of her head!'

Ellen was scornful. 'That doesn't mean anything. They all say that.'

'What better disguise could an alien have than to be Mrs Warren?' Serena reasoned.

The little group stirred anxiously and for a moment they were silent.

'You won't catch me falling asleep in her lessons any more!' Daniel decided.

There was a general murmur of agreement.

'But she knows all that stuff about history,' argued Ellen stubbornly. 'She can't have just popped from out of a pod.'

'Well, she didn't even know the difference between a discovery and an invasion!' Evelyn sneered.

'Yeah,' said Serena. 'The Martians probably think they're discovering the Earth.'

Ellen gave in. 'Okay, I believe you, but what can we do about it?'

Everyone looked at Evelyn expectantly. After all, she was the expert.

'I don't know,' Evelyn confessed. 'I fell asleep at the end of the film.'

'Perhaps we should tell a teacher,' suggested Daniel.

'Never!' cried Serena. 'For all we know, they could all have been taken over by the alien plant invasion.'

The group quickly split into two factions; those who wanted to go home, as Rowan put it, 'Right now,' and those who wished to save the planet and strike back with weed killer and garden shears.

Evelyn remembered some nonviolent ways of dealing with plants and aliens.

'I've got two ideas,' she announced.

'We'll try them both,' said Serena loyally. 'Better safe than sorry.'

Evelyn frowned. 'We can't,' she snapped. 'Let me explain. The first idea is that, basically, Mrs Warren is an alien plant, isn't she?'

'Okay, okay, we agree she's a plant,' interrupted Ellen.

'Well our plants at home get droopy and wither if I forget to water them. Maybe, if we can stop Mrs Warren from getting to any water, you know, make sure she doesn't drink anything at all, then she'll have to go back to Mars and we'll get the real Mrs Warren back!'

'What's the other idea?' asked Daniel, unimpressed. Evelyn was embarrassed.

'Well, the second plan is based on the fact that Mrs Warren is an alien monster, right?'

'Yes, yes we know,' muttered Rowan.

'Well in The Blob, another science fiction film I saw once, they tried everything, but there was only one way to destroy the monster.'

'Yes?' encouraged Serena, hopefully.

'They had to squirt all this water at it...'

There was a pause.

'So your advice,' said Ellen coldly, 'is to pour water on her, OR not pour water on her. Now why didn't I think of that?'

'Shut up!' said Serena.

They voted on Evelyn's two ideas and chose the second plan. Then, as no one could be found to volunteer to douse Mrs Warren with water, they unanimously chose the first plan.

Upstairs in the school staffroom, the object of the children's anxious debate, Mrs Warren, was once again standing at the window. Finally, with a sigh of despair, she removed first a right, and then a left contact lens from her painfully watering eyes.

'It's completely hopeless,' she sighed. 'I'm taking these lenses back to the opticians. They irritate my eyes so much that I spend all my time blinking.'

Miss Balaswara looked up from the pile of mathematics papers she was marking.

'You've only tried them for one morning, Carol. I'm sure you'll get used to them in time, and you look so different without them!'

'Nonsense!' cried Mrs Warren, making Miss Balaswara jump and forget the marks she had just painstakingly totalled. 'No one even noticed, unless you count a couple of girls from class Two B who stared at me as if I'd grown two heads!'

Miss Balaswara smiled sympathetically. 'Now, now. I expect they were just admiring the way you look without your glasses.'

'Well they can admire the way I look without my contact lenses from now on, because I've had enough of them.'

It was clear Mrs Warren had made up her mind, so with a brief, disapproving shrug, Miss Balaswara returned to marking her maths papers. A short while later, Mrs Warren rose and left, without her glasses or her contact lenses, for her dinner duties; leaving Miss Balaswara shaking her head as she picked up the waste-paper basket her colleague had unwittingly kicked over.

Teachers on dinner duty were expected to combine their dinner time with supervising the pupils. Mrs Warren sat down at the first table she came to and soon found herself joined by Evelyn and Serena. Her slightly unfocused smile of greeting drew a strange, sickly grin from Serena. Evelyn made no attempt to disguise a scowl of deep distrust. Mrs Warren was about to make a sprightly comment about her hopes for an improved quality of history homework, but it seemed to dry in her throat.

'Er,..pass me the water jug, please, Serena. I'm parched,' she said.

Even to Mrs Warren's imperfect vision, it appeared that the two girls shuddered.

'Sorry,' said Evelyn, her scowl abruptly replaced by a sweetly, earnest expression. 'You won't want to drink this water.'

Mrs Warren's eyebrows rose and Serena gripped the water jug protectively to her chest.

'Serena's just dropped something in the jug...er...by accident,' Evelyn continued, staring meaningfully at her friend.

'That's right,' said Serena, hastily plunging her arm up to her elbow into the water jug. 'A charm from my charm bracelet fell in,' she explained.

'But you aren't wearing a charm bracelet, Serena,' the teacher pointed out.

There was a long pause, Serena smiled ingratiatingly,

'We're not supposed to wear jewellery at school Mrs Warren,' she said brightly.

Mrs Warren's look of amazement was replaced by an ominous frown. To avoid further discussion, Evelyn pulled Serena to her feet and took the water jug away from her.

'Her hand looks a bit grimy, Miss. I'd better go and throw this water out. You go and wash your hands, Serena.'

'Remember to bring some water back with you!' Mrs Warren called after them.

The girls were faced with a moral dilemma. Returning with water might be helping an alien invade the earth, but if they did not return they would certainly miss dinner.

'I'm starving,' said Evelyn as they headed towards the water trolley, where Rowan and Lily had posted themselves on guard duty.

'Mrs Warren sent us to get her some water and we can't go back and have our dinner without it,' said Serena bluntly.

Lily, who had already eaten, did not see that there was any problem. 'It's only cheese and egg flan today. Really yukky. You wouldn't have liked it anyway.'

Evelyn and Serena refused to be consoled by her offer of bubble gum. Tempers threatened to flare. At this point Rowan offered them, what she quite accurately called, a solution. She had been busily unscrewing salt cellars taken from some tables near by. She now emptied their contents into a fresh jug of water which she exchanged for the one Evelyn had.

'See how she likes that,' she smirked.

Privately, Serena thought that an alien plant from Mars would probably lap it up, but she was too hungry to want to discuss the matter. When Serena returned from washing her hands, Mrs Warren was staring with unmistakable disgust at a glass of water poured from the replacement jug. A swirling current of undissolved, white crystals was obvious to the poorest vision.

'What on earth is that?' she asked ferociously.

Dan, Ellen, Ebony, and Serena peered into the glass and then looked inquiringly at Evelyn.

'What's what?' asked Evelyn innocently.

The teacher rubbed her eyes. Her suspicious, but ill-focused gaze travelled from the jug to Evelyn and back to the glass. The children held their breath in suspense as she stood up, pushed her uneaten dinner neatly away and stalked out of the dining room.

Mrs Warren continued to be dogged by mishaps for the rest of the day. During afternoon break, an attempt to sip a cup of tea as she patrolled the yard on playground duty was abruptly terminated by a direct hit from a football. Her cup was then swiftly borne away, never to return. It had been snatched from her amid a flurry of apologies, by a small group of children who, she noticed, included both Evelyn Henry and Serena Adebola. Stranger still was the emergency fire drill, mysteriously triggered off just as she was looking forward to a nice cup of coffee in the staff room.

At nine o'clock the following morning, the school playground was the usual scene of hustle and bustle and early morning faces. Morale, however, was at an all time low among the small band who had aimed to hold back the alien invasion of Earth.

The general feeling in the group was that Mrs Warren, the alien, looked no more defeated when last seen at hometime than she had looked at first sighting in Two B's history lesson. After a brief bout of whispering between Serena and herself, Evelyn stepped forward to make an announcement.

'The time has come, brothers and sisters, to fight fire with fire.'

'Water,' hissed Serena urgently.

Evelyn ignored the interruption and continued. 'The time is right to try Plan B. When Mrs Warren comes in, I will throw the water at her and she will disintegrate! Because this is a dangerous mission, Serena will divert her attention by pretending to be asleep. While the alien is trying to copy Serena's body with a pod, I can surprise her with the water.'

The group were impressed by the daring of the scheme. Although they were not all convinced of its logic, it seemed the kind of thing that ought to work. Evelyn ran off to get some water and Serena stretched out on a dry patch of playground floor within clear view of the staff entrance. The rest of the group were to mill around and prevent her from being seen until the right moment. Dan was on the look out. At a signal from him, the crowd would part and Serena would attract attention by snoring until Evelyn sprang out with the water.

At five past nine, Mrs Warren, normally a committed and enthusiastic teacher, made her way to school in a mood of deep despondency. Although outwardly she seemed her usual spruce and upright self, inside she felt as dejected and wilting as any alien plant fighter could hope for. Gone was all attempt at updating her appearance by wearing contact lenses. She had returned for comfort to her heavily framed, but reliable old glasses.

As she walked towards the school building, she mused sadly on the events of the previous day. She didn't understand children and she feared she never would. She was a failure. She couldn't control them. She couldn't even get one of the girls to fetch a clean jug of water. She felt as if she only had to look at a child to produce the most bizarre and wayward behaviour. With these thoughts, she turned through the staff entrance. In the next instant, all thought was scattered by the sight that met her astonished gaze. Amid a half circle of apparently heedless schoolmates, Serena Adebola lay spreadeagled across the yard. Her eyes were closed and a raucous grunt was emitted from her mouth with each breath.

'Good grief,' the teacher gasped, 'she's having a fit!'

Within seconds she had darted across the yard. She removed her jacket and rolled it up to make a cushion which she tucked carefully under Serena's head.

At the first touch of Mrs Warren's hands, Serena stiffened with fear. She opened her eyes and was relieved to see the familiar face of her teacher peering out from behind her heavy framed glasses. This was not the Mrs Warren of yesterday. There was something unmistakably human in the look of concern in her teacher's face. They had done it! The alien had been forced out by lack of water and now Mrs Warren was herself again. Then, for the second time that morning, Serena stiffened with fear. Looming behind her kneeling teacher was Evelyn, carrying a jug full of water that she had sneaked out of the dining room. Mrs Warren turned to see what she was looking at.

'It's Mrs Warren,' yelped Serena. 'It's *really* her. She's come back.'

Evelyn was caught with her arms raised, holding the jug ready to dash the water over the woman below.

'Oh what a good idea. You've brought some water for your friend. Actually, I don't think she'll need it now,' said Mrs Warren, smiling up at Evelyn. Reluctantly, Evelyn lowered the jug. She stared intently at her teacher. Serena was right, this was the real Mrs Warren. Her heart leapt. What a triumph. She had saved the day after all!

'I'm so glad to see you, Mrs Warren. We were so frightened!' Evelyn beamed.

The rest of the group thronged around congratulating Evelyn and Serena and patting Mrs Warren on the back. They weren't quite sure how it had happened, but they were proud of themselves.

'Good old Mrs Warren!'

Mrs Warren helped Serena back to her feet. She was at the centre of the excited and friendly crowd. It was all very pleasant, but rather mystifying at the same time. Serena had made a miraculously fast and thorough recovery. Her schoolmates, who had appeared totally unconcerned when she lay groaning and unconscious at their feet, with the exception of Evelyn, were all obviously thrilled and delighted now that she was better. Yesterday, they had all seemed hostile and unruly and yet today it was clear they were pleased to see her and were touchingly grateful for her attentions to their friend. She could see she had quite misjudged them. Children are so sensible, sweet and straightforward when you really understand them, she thought.

THE FIGHT

KIM HENDRY

It's the last lesson before lunch. English.

'Huh-hmm!'

Jasmine's head jerks up. 'Sorry, Miss?' she says, flushing slightly.

The teacher purses her small, dry lips.

'I didn't say anything, Jasmine, but with your head buried so deeply in that book you're reading, I don't suppose you were listening.' Her voice grows colder. 'Were you?'

Jasmine shrugs helplessly, her olive cheeks fiery. 'No,' she admits.

'No,' Mrs Vonnegut agrees. 'Instead of getting on with the work I've set for everyone, including you, you were reading a book! Is there any particular...'

'I've *finished* it,' Jasmine interrupts.

'I beg your pardon?'

'I said I've finished the work you set,' Jasmine repeats, an insolent edge to her voice. As she stares defiantly into the teacher's eyes, Jasmine can hear snorts of laughter coming from behind, and her pride bristles. So *what* if nobody likes her? That doesn't mean some rickety, old woman can pick on her, make a fool of her.

'You've finished, have you?' Mrs Vonnegut allows herself a small, sarcastic smile. 'And, of course, it didn't occur to you to ask me to get you some more work. No...that's far too normal a reaction for you. *You* have to be different. You have to be special.'

The unfairness of the attack hurts and infuriates Jasmine. It isn't her fault she's had to come to this school. She didn't want to move from Ealing, from her friends, her dog, her stepfather; leave the familiar streets of her childhood and memories. That was all her mother's idea. And it certainly isn't Jasmine's fault that the lessons here are all so boring. The teachers spend all their time explaining what she already knows and setting work that she's already done at St. Angela's. When Jasmine told them this, perhaps rather bluntly, they seemed to take it as a personal humiliation. Well, that was her mother's explanation.

'Well?' Mrs Vonnegut raps. 'What's going on in that odd little mind of yours?'

Jasmine is fuming at her words but as she opens her mouth to speak, a voice behind her sneers: 'A pile of rubbish...'cos that's what comes out when she opens her mouth!'

Jasmine's entire body stiffens with rage. Twisting round in her seat, she turns to face the girl she has come to loathe with her whole being. Tossie Thompson.

'Why don't you go back to London Zoo with all the other animals!' she screams.

Tossie's mouth falls open for a moment then she jumps up from her seat and kicks her chair back. 'Come here and *make* me,' she taunts, her short, square knuckles resting aggressively on her hips.

'Okay, I will!' Furious, Jasmine stands up. 'I'm sick to death of you and your stupidness. You're always picking on me, ever since I got here!' Jasmine swallows hard. 'I never asked to come to this rubbish tip of a school; and I never asked to be put in this class.' Her anger is turning her tongue into a vicious sword. '...And I don't see why I should have to endure listening to a spiteful, little wretch like you! You're ugly, you're stupid and you smell.'

She gasps as Tossie leans over her desk and grabs a bunch of Jasmine's hair, tugging hard.

Jasmine raises her arm, to fight off Tossie's grip, only to have it grasped from behind by a bony hand.

'Sit down!' exclaims Mrs Vonnegut, '...before I throw you out...both of you.' She glares at them. 'I will not have this kind of disturbance in my class. Fight outside if you must, but not in my class.' She glances round the room. 'That applies to all of you. Do you understand?'

Sullen silence.

Jasmine sits down noisily, her head hammering with anger. She can feel the unfriendly stare of twenty four pairs of eyes boring into her back, laughing at her. She juts out her chin, ignoring them but it's no use; the class's mood has changed, she can feel it. Excitement fills the air. They want a fight.

A new wave of prickly heat washes over Jasmine as her straining ears pick up the mutterings and goadings that drift from the back of the class.

'Show her, Tossie.'

'Teach her a lesson, man!'

'Stuck up cow!'

She sneaks a look at her watch. Three quarters of an hour to go. As the minutes tick by, Jasmine's impetuous anger begins to drain. In its place, a cold dread in the very pit of her stomach.

Brrring. Jasmine's stomach lurches sickeningly as the dinner bell rings. Chairs scrape back and feet hurry for the door as she busies herself putting pens and the troublesome book away. 'Don't let them be waiting for me,' she prays, her fingers suddenly clumsy.

She looks up. About twenty of her classmates stand crowded around the door and there is no mistaking the expression on their faces. Out of the corner of her eye, Jasmine watches Mrs Vonnegut, a shaming plea trembling on her tongue. 'Surely she's seen them? She knows they're all against me,' thinks Jasmine. 'Why doesn't she do something?'

Pride and stubbornness battle with the silent words, as Mrs Vonnegut sweeps from the room, ignoring the children outside. Jasmine walks slowly to the door, forcing herself to meet Tossie's dark stare.

'Go on, Tossie,' a hand thrusts the girl forward.

'I'm sick of you,' she shouts into Jasmine's face, 'coming to this school. Thinking you're some big deal. You'll realise you don't say things like that to me and get away with it!' Her eyes burn with fury. She glances at her friends to gauge their support.

'Animals,' Jasmine thinks, sickened, staring into their livid, gloating faces. 'They just want to see me get battered.' Her body suddenly feeling strange and rubbery.

'You reckon you're so damn brainy!' Tossie hisses.

'...and so-o-o good looking!' another voice drawled, scornfully.

Samantha and Miriam, giggling, nudge each other, flicking back their hair with exaggerated gestures.

'I don't do that,' Jasmine turns on them hotly.

'I don't do that,' they mimic in unison. Tossie laughs.

'Yes you do; but let me tell you, girl, nobody'll think you're pretty when I'm finished with you. You'll look like Quasimodo.'

'She's only skinny,' Tossie's friend, Sally, adds, kicking Jasmine's ankle.

'Look at her, she couldn't beat up a flea!' Someone circles Jasmine's arm with cruel fingers.

'Jasmine,' says Tossie pityingly, 'be at the Green Gate in five minutes and then we'll see who belongs in the zoo.' Her voice roughening at the remembered insult. Turning on her heel, she swaggers off down the stairs, followed by the rowdy crowd.

Jasmine stares after them. Her lips quiver but she bites them viciously. The terror of crying is a thousand times greater than her present fear. She tries to think of a way out but her mind panics, as she trudges slowly down the steps, her steps drawing her closer and closer against her will.

'It's not Tossie I'm afraid of,' Jasmine assures herself. 'I could beat her up. It's fighting in front of everybody. When I know they all hate me. Nobody's on my side.'

She walks out from the protection of the building to where the small crowd waits. When they see Jasmine, they begin to chant: 'Fight! Fight! Fight! Fight!' Jasmine's legs falter but she forces herself on.

'They all love a fight when it's not them,' Jasmine thinks, bitterly. Even the few people she got on well with were crowded around Tossie, chattering excitedly.

As Jasmine approaches, Tossie struts up to her, cheered on by the others.

'Mash her up, man. Teach her a lesson!'

She laughs hysterically into Jasmine's face, pushes her roughly and jumps back into the road.

The crowd let out a roar.

All at once, Jasmine's earlier rage comes flooding back. Her hands begin to tingle. She rushes at Tossie, slapping her face and grabbing her hair in great handfuls. Tossie retaliates by thrusting her fingers into Jasmine's tangled curls, tearing at the roots. They struggle along the road, locked in combat like two small, wiry wrestlers.

'Tossie!...Tossie!...Tossie!' yell her classmates.

Their voices ring only distantly in Jasmine's ears. Her head is stuck under Tossie's arm and she is wriggling desperately to break free, her face scarlet.

At one point, Jasmine's ankle twists and she stumbles and falls heavily to the ground. Tossie tumbles on top of her and they roll around savagely. Jasmine can feel Tossie scratching her neck; feels her tough little body grunt and shudder. Her head bangs against a parked car. A grown-up shouts from a window but doesn't come out. Spiteful feet kick Jasmine from behind.

'Leave her alone, Sally,' someone orders. 'Let them get on with it.'

Jasmine has stopped thinking. It's all happening too fast, but her body's instinct warns her to keep on top. She manages to trip Tossie and they fall further into the road.

Suddenly there is a squeal of brakes and the shriek of tyres scraping the tarmac. A door slams. Footsteps thunder towards them and a voice bellows down:

'You blasted kids! What d'you think you're doing, fighting like a couple of alley cats in the middle of the road. I could've killed yer! Get on up and out of my way.'

Jasmine and Tossie blink as a pair of giant hands reach down and drag them to their feet. They stand, panting and grimy, glaring at each other.

'Well?' The man folds brawny, spam-coloured arms across a massive chest. He turns and scowls at the crowd staring resentfully at him. 'Go on — scram!'

Slowly they turn and leave, muttering rudely.

The man turns to Jasmine, who now stands alone.

'Are you alright, love?' His rough tone softens slightly.

She nods mutely and after a moment, he gets back into his car and roars off.

The midday sun burns. Jasmine, wearily, crumples onto the hot pavement. Sinking her sore face into grubby, pink palms, she begins to cry.

'Why didn't I just keep my big mouth shut? Why, why, why?'

The fight had been brewing for days, but her stupid, stubborn pride wouldn't let Jasmine ignore Tossie's taunts. It had really all started on the very first day. Jasmine had walked into the boisterous classroom, noting, with dismay, that the teacher had not turned up yet. She was rigid with shyness but hid it beneath a blank, bored gaze. Sitting down at an empty wooden desk, she had stared at her new classmates, shouting and chasing each other, jumping up onto the tables. Then Tossie, surrounded by a group of her friends, had leaned across and said loudly to Jasmine: 'You're not very *talkative*, are you?' It was meant as a friendly gesture, Jasmine realized afterwards, but, at the time, it had sounded painfully sarcastic to her ears and her edgy temper had flared up:

'Why should I want to talk to you?' Boring. Defensive. Untrue.

From this small disagreement the big hatred had grown. Tossie had obviously decided that Jasmine was stuck up and unfriendly and had begun to taunt her. She was the loudest girl in the class and many of the other kids took her lead. Jasmine responded with clever, sarcastic remarks, refusing to show her hurt.

Her mother told her: 'Just ignore them and they'll soon grow tired of teasing you. Then they'll leave you alone. Half the problem is that you're so touchy and when you're upset, you simply lash out.'

'But they hate me, they really do!' Jasmine protested.

Her mother shrugged. 'The point is that if you always get mad at something Tossie or one of the others, says, then they'll keep on doing it, because they know they're going to get a reaction. In future, don't give them that satisfaction.'

It's one o'clock. Jasmine waits outside the classroom door after lunch. She hugs her bag to her chest, a useless defence.

'...if he hadn't come, you would've battered her good...'

'...did you see how much hair Tossie pulled from her head? I bet she's as bald as Kojak!' Screams of laughter.

Jasmine's heart thumps uncomfortably. She forces herself to look at the peeling poster opposite, as they tumble around the corner.

'Jasmine!' Tossie grins. She walks up to Jasmine, peering insolently into her face. Two pairs of brown eyes stare at each other.

Tossie pokes a finger about an inch from Jasmine's cheek. 'Look, a black eye!' she exclaims triumphantly. Jasmine angrily slaps her hand away, as people laugh and jeer.

'You should've broken her nose while you were at it, Tossie,' Sally says with a spiteful smirk. Jasmine looks at her pink face and straggly, mousey hair with hatred.

'Look at her, looking down her nose at me,' Sally complains. 'That's your problem, Jasmine, you think you're just too good. We're sick and tired of your stuck-up ways, so you'd better watch out,' says Tossie.

Jasmine watches her basking in the attention, scornful words trembling on her lips. A terrible loneliness clenches her insides tight, and a jagged lump swells in her throat.

'If ever that girl lays another finger on me, I'll kill her,' she vows.

Jasmine's mind toys with the gruesome possibilities. She sees herself pushing Tossie under a big, red double-decker, and imagines the horrible squelch: or setting fire to Tossie with a bunsen burner in the school lab. Her greasy hair should be highly inflammable!

The next lesson, Geography, has the usual chaos that 1B brings to most of its classes. Mr Mustafa wrings his hands and begs for order. This generally lasts about five minutes before his pupils erupt into another orgy of disobedience. Today is worse than ever. Everybody is talking about the fight. The few who weren't there, eagerly lapping up the details.

Jasmine sits alone by the window, unable to shut out the jokes and the laughter and jeers. 'I *didn't* get beaten up!' she wants to shout, but her throat is too tight with hot, salty tears.

It is the loneliest and longest ninety minutes of Jasmine's life. Worse even than when Daniel and her mother split up. 'How could I ever have wanted to be friends with this bunch of oafs?' Jasmine thinks. 'I hate them. All of them. If they all got down on their hands and knees and *begged* to be my friend, I'd kick them in the teeth!'

The minutes crawl past, slower than a snail. 'After this lesson, there's still Biology to get through.' Gradually, the idea of staying until three-thirty grows intolerable. Jasmine has to get out, leave, escape from these stifling four walls.

'Maybe I won't come back,' she thinks.

When the bell rings, Jasmine's bag is already packed. She marches across the room and out the door, her clammy eyes downcast. They all stare at her but she just keeps on walking. Down the stairs. Across the hall. Out the main entrance. Past the playing fields and finally; through the gates. Jasmine almost shudders with relief. Free!

She heads straight for the high street. People jostle her on the busy pavement. A twelve year old girl, invisible in this adult world. Jasmine walks for hours, her only real thought to get as far away as possible from school.

Jasmine stops at an ice-cream van, and buys a coke and a hot-dog. The smells of mustard, ketchup, fried onions and juicy frankfurter are almost unbearable for her empty, grumbling stomach. Walking along, she bites hungrily into the food, hardly chewing the steaming bun. Further on, she purchases several bars of chocolate and some packets of biscuit.

Gradually, the grimy, grey tower blocks give way to larger, red brick houses, then green fields and distant hills, ripened almost yellow by the sun.

The overwhelming loneliness Jasmine felt earlier has been replaced by a grim, muted misery and exhaustion.

She looks at her watch for the first time since that afternoon. Ten past eight. God, she must have been walking for almost six hours! Sitting down on a wooden bench, Jasmine leans back. Every part of her body aches. Shoulder, back, knees, feet. They all feel stiff and sore.

She rubs the heel of her hands in her gravelly eyes, trying to think what to do. 'I must be miles from home,' she thinks. She examines herself to see if she feels nervous about going back home and facing her mother, but there's no leaping heart. Nothing.

'That shows how much I'm suffering,' Jasmine tells herself.

She sits for a while longer. Then she gets up and hobbles across the road to where a woman is just climbing out of her car.

'Excuse me.' Jasmine clears her throat. 'Excuse me. Can you tell me what area this is?'

The woman looks faintly surprised. 'Er, yes. You're in Barnet.'

'And can you tell me where the nearest 'phone box is?'

The woman raises a bulky, freckled arm. 'Turn left at the corner and carry on walking for about five minutes. You can't miss it. Have...'

'Thanks,' Jasmine breaks in and turns away, too tired for explanations.

She trudges towards the 'phone box, stepping under its plastic roof. Wearily, her hands pull the purse from her jumbled bag. She scatters the coins on top of the 'phone directories, places a ten pence piece in the slot and presses the numbers.

The tone begins to ring. Suddenly, Jasmine is overcome by fierce longing for her mother; to cry in her arms and be rocked and cradled.

'I want to go home.'

A woman's husky, urgent voice answers the phone.

'Hello?'

'Hi Mum, it's me,' says Jasmine, starting to cry. 'I want to come home.'

ONE TO FETCH HELP

CAROLINE WORSLEY

Helen was worried, but this was not unusual. Helen was worried about getting lost. She was one of those people who could get lost walking around the block or even down a straight road! She could never seem to remember which direction anywhere was. She wondered, if she put her hand up just once more and told Mrs Morrison that she was worried, if her teacher would be able to reassure her; not only tell her that there was nothing to worry about, but make her feel there really was nothing to worry about.

'Well,' Mrs Morrison was saying, '...if there are no more questions.'

Helen's hand shot up. This was her last chance.

'Mrs Morrison, suppose we get lost?'

The whole class groaned and many of them raised their eyes to the ceiling as if this curious behaviour could rid them of Helen's incessant concerns. Mrs Morrison looked at Helen over the top of her glasses and Helen knew that she had chosen the wrong moment and had asked the wrong question. She wished that she could be lost right now.

'Helen,' said Mrs Morrison slowly, with a sigh in her voice, '...what are you going to be taking with you tomorrow? Apart from your packed lunch, your extra sweater, your sun hat, in case it's sunny, your anorak, in case it rains and endless packets of sweets, which I know you'll all take with you even though you've been told they're bad for your teeth.'

Her eyes swept round the class taking in all the guilty looks of those who had planned just this.

'What else, Helen? What else?'

'A map, Mrs Morrison.' Helen's stomach felt as though it had dropped down to her knees.

'And...'

'A compass.' It made a further lurch down her shins.

'And...'

'A whistle.' Surely it couldn't go beyond her ankles. It had fallen so far that it had taken her voice with it and only a squeak came out.

Mrs Morrison came to her rescue. She smiled and said reassuringly, 'And a watch and all your instructions and plans and, most important of all, two friends. You know where you're going. You know what you've got to do, and none of you will be on your own.'

She dismissed the class and they left excitedly, pushing and shoving each other in the cloakroom as if that would make tomorrow come sooner. Tomorrow 4M were going on an outing. This, in itself, was not unusual. Nearly every week during the summer term, a coach pulled up outside the school to take a group of children somewhere, but tomorrow's outing was different. The coach would be coming for them in the morning, just as usual, but instead of all going somewhere together, they were going to be dropped off, in threes, at different points in the forest. Armed with their maps and compasses and whistles and watches and instructions and plans and their packed lunches and extra sweaters and sunhats and anoraks and endless packets of sweets, they had all day to make their way to a central point where Mrs Morrison and some of their parents would be waiting for them. When everyone had arrived they would fry sausages and burgers over a campfire, talk about their day's adventures to anyone who would listen and then all go home again.

The children had been supplied with large scale maps of the forest; the sort which show all the footpaths and mileposts and individual fields and fences. They had planned their own routes and written sets of instructions for their group, which Mrs Morrison had checked through to make sure that they had got things right. Each trio had to complete a walk of about five or six miles and they had all been training. Once around the school field was about four hundred metres. Fifteen hundred metres was roughly a mile, so if you walked around...well, quite a lot of times, then you'd have covered the distance they had to walk tomorrow.

Helen wasn't worried about the walking, she did plenty of that with her mum and dad at the weekends. Helen's father would take the map and stride off in front while Helen and her mother followed behind. Her knowledge of the countryside was considerable but she never knew where she was going. She just looked for the reassuring figure of her father and followed that.

Her friend Jane wasn't worried about the walking. Although a lot of her time was spent helping her mother look after her younger brothers and sisters, she had recently taken up jogging, and several evenings a week she did a round trip of the estate where they lived.

The third member of Helen and Jane's group had been hard to find. Helen and Jane were a pair, and a very close pair. Ever since they'd started in the Infants on the same day they'd been inseparable. They worked together, played together, shared the contents of their lunch boxes and got into trouble together. When Mrs Morrison said that they would have to work in threes to prepare for the outing, they had asked if they could be a twos instead. Mrs Morrison had said no, just in case one of them got hurt, while they were in the forest, they had to have one to stay with the injured person and one to fetch help. So they had asked Lucy to join them.

Lucy had only recently moved into the area and come to their school. She was a quiet girl who kept herself to herself. They thought she wouldn't be any trouble.

'Yes,' said Mrs Morrison, for what seemed like the hundredth time, 'we are still going.' She glanced out of the class room window. 'The forecast says no more rain until this evening, so we should be all right.'

The register was called, compasses and whistles handed out, maps and instructions were packed. The coach arrived and they all scrambled aboard and were off.

The forest was not far away but the morning traffic in the town held them up. At last they reached the point where the first group was to start their walk. By ten thirty all the children had been dropped off and the sun had come out. Helen and Jane, and Lucy, had waved goodbye as they entered the forest.

The first part of their route was easy; about a mile or so up a straight wide ride between two plantations of conifers.

'Even you can't get lost here,' laughed Jane.

Helen kept quiet. She did not even want to think of such things at the moment. The two friends walked along together, while Lucy walked in silence behind them. It seemed to her that they scarcely realized that she was there. Every now and then one of them would break off from talking and laughing to turn around and check, but Lucy felt that if there had been a cardboard cut-out of her there, it would have satisfied them. They didn't really want to know if she was there. In fact, they would have been happier if she had not been.

Just before eleven o'clock they reached the crossroads where they had to turn off the main ride and take a narrower path to the left. It seemed as if they had been walking for ages.

'We might as well have lunch really,' said Jane. 'I mean it's nearly lunch time and then we won't have to carry it any more.'

Helen and Jane put their lunchboxes together, as they did

at school every day, and helped themselves to whatever they fancied. Lucy sat on her own.

When they'd nearly finished Helen said, 'Oh, Lucy. Would you like to share your lunch with us?'

As she looked into her own, almost empty lunchbox, she realized what a silly thing this was to say.

'It's all right,' said Lucy, as she snapped her box shut and packed it into her rucksack. She had known this wasn't going to be a good day and she had been right. The best thing would be to get going so that they could reach the meeting place as soon as possible.

'Come on,' she said. 'Or we'll never get there.'

She hoisted her rucksack onto her back and set off along the new pathway. The other two scrambled to their feet, feeling guilty now at having left Lucy out of things. They stowed their belongings away quickly and hurried after her. Lucy was carrying the group's map and as she strode ahead of the other two, they felt somehow that she was taking their security with her.

'Don't go so fast, Lou,' called Helen. Keeping up with Lucy's pace was already giving her a stitch.

'Well, there's no point in hanging about,' said Lucy, over her shoulder. 'It looks as if it's going to pour with rain again.'

'She's right,' said Jane to Helen, speaking quietly so that Lucy would not hear her. She nodded towards the black sky, lit with that curious brightness that heralds a downpour. Helen looked up from her stooped position and she had to agree.

Lucy suddenly stopped. She had been studying the map as she marched along. She turned abruptly to the right and held her arm out in front of her as if she was pointing the way.

'I think we'll go through here,' she said. 'It'll be quicker. It's a sort of short cut.' She started to go into the woodland on their right hand side.

'Hang on,' called Jane, alarmed. 'We can't do that. Mrs

Morrison said we must keep to our route. We've made a plan and we've got to stick to it.'

'Afraid you'll get lost or something?' sneered Lucy.

At the word 'lost', Helen's stomach gave a lurch.

'Well,' continued Lucy, 'I say we go this way. And...' she left the path and entered the undergrowth, '...I've got the map.'

Before the others could stop her she was off, darting through the bushes, ducking branches, jumping brambles. For the first time that day she felt good. She'd show those two, no-time-for-anyone-else, do-share-our-empty-lunchboxes, ever-such-good-friends.

'Lucy, wait. Don't go so fast.'

'Lucy. We shouldn't. Remember the plan.'

Remember the plan! What plan? Lucy had had no part in planning it. Those two had decided which way they wanted to go and she'd had to agree. Well, now she, Lucy, was deciding which way they'd go. The feeling of power that her action had brought her gave strength to her legs. She charged through the forest as if nothing could stop her. She knew she ought to look at the map again but she was afraid the others might catch up with her and try to make her turn back. She tried to keep going in a straight line but with bushes and trees in the way she had to keep weaving from side to side. If only the sun was still out she could use it as a guide, but the sky was just a glowing greyness. She struggled to remember what the map looked like. She judged they must have come nearly two miles from the path now, so quite soon they should meet another one, unless they'd gone too far to the left. In which case they would miss the path and she was not quite sure where they would end up. She screwed up her eyes in an effort to visualize the map. Wham! There was a terrible pain in her head and then she saw the fallen leaves on the ground coming up slowly, ever so slowly, to meet her. She seemed to bounce as she hit the ground and then she lay absolutely still.

'She's dead,' said Helen, clutching Jane's arm as they looked down, panting, at their companion.

There was purple bruising on her forehead and her eyes looked sunken in her bloodless face. A wisp of breath escaped from her mouth and Helen and Jane sank to their knees beside her. Lucy's eyes opened and she looked out at them as if from some faraway place.

'Lie still,' commanded Jane. 'You've had a nasty hit on the head. You shouldn't move.' Lucy moaned and closed her eyes again. Helen drew back. She could not bear to see anyone in pain. She knew that she would not be able to bring herself to touch her, but Jane was already easing her into a more comfortable position. She took her anorak out of her rucksack and then it started to rain; great big, lazy, blobs of water that burst as they hit the ground.

After the first few minutes of enthusiastic downpour, the rain settled to a steady summer drizzle. Helen and Jane looked at each other. This was the occasion that had not been planned for. There was nothing in their notes to tell them what to do now. 'Stick to the paths,' Mrs Morrison had said, '...then if you don't turn up at the meeting place, we can send out a search party for you.' Stick to the paths! They'd gone deep into the forest itself. How far? A mile? Two miles? How could a search party find them here?

'We'll have to go and get help,' said Jane.

'But we can't leave Lucy. We might not find her again.'

'One to stay with the injured and one to fetch help. You can see why we had to be in threes,' said Jane.

'If we'd been just us two, this wouldn't have happened,' said Helen.

They looked down at Lucy and began to realize that if they hadn't treated her so badly, this wouldn't have happened.

Jane picked up the sodden map that had fallen from Lucy's hand when she hit the tree. As she opened it up, it started to tear along the creases.

'Do you know where we are?' asked Helen. The two of them pored over the map and traced their path along the main ride, turning left, along the narrower path and then into the woodland, but how far in? It was hard to tell. They had not yet come across another path. Looking at the map, they could see what Lucy was trying to achieve. It would be a short cut to the meeting place, but it would also be possible to miss the meeting place altogether.

'Look,' said Jane, '...I think I'd better go and see if I can find help. I mean...well, you know, you're always worried about getting...'

'Don't say it,' said Helen, so fiercely that her friend was taken aback. 'No. You must stay here with Lucy. You know much more about looking after people than I do. I'll go and get help.'

She started to pick up her things as she spoke. She was afraid that her friend might make her stay with Lucy, poor hurt Lucy who she would not be able to touch. Although she was frightened of getting lost, the terror waiting for her in the unknown forest seemed less than the terror of staying where she was.

'All right,' said Jane, surprised at the determination in Helen's voice. 'I'll stay here.'

Helen picked up the map. 'I'll make my way back to the path where we turned off, and then go on the way we meant to go. It might take longer, but at least that way I won't get...well, I should be able to find the way.'

Jane gave her friend a quick hug and then Helen was gone. The undergrowth swallowed her up and Jane turned back to Lucy and settled down to wait.

Helen had not been going long when she realized that she did not know if she was going in the right direction or not. She came to a particularly thick tangle of brambles and made her way round it. She stumbled on, ducking under low branches. She came to a place where there seemed to be no way through at all, so she turned back to try and find another route. She suddenly realized that she had absolutely no idea which direction she had been trying to go in. She turned round, hoping she might recognize the way she had come. All around her the trees, the bushes, the brambles, looked the same. She turned the other way, hoping it would make a difference, and inside her she felt a rising pressure that seemed as if it would squeeze every last breath out of her body. She had to scream. Perhaps someone would hear her. She opened her mouth, but no sound came out except for an almost silent gasp. Suddenly her breath was released in rapid gusts that racked her body and she felt hot tears rolling down her cheeks. 'Jane. Somebody. Help!' she sobbed.

She had thought she knew what it was like to be worried. Nearly every day she was worried about something, but someone always came to her rescue. Never before had she felt such complete and utter hopelessness. Her feeling of inadequacy meant that she could not fully understand her situation. She was filled with panic; consumed by anxiety. There was nothing she could do but sit in a crumpled heap and sob.

For a short while crying was an active relief. It made her feel as if she was doing something, but she soon realized that there was no friend at hand to cheer her up, no father in front for her to follow, no teacher to tell her what to do. What else? What else? What else? She remembered the previous afternoon in class when she had asked Mrs Morrison what would happen if they got lost. Mrs Morrison had gone on and on about all the things they would have with them. What else? A map. A compass. A whistle. The map was not much good if she didn't know where she was. Jane had the compass because she was the only one who knew how to use it properly. But, Helen had a whistle. She thrust her hands into her jeans pockets and almost started to cry again as her fingers closed around the reassuring shape. She put it to her lips. Six short blasts for an emergency, but she was so relieved to have something to do that she emptied her lungs six times into the whistle. She sat down, out of breath, half expecting someone to appear through the undergrowth immediately.

As her panic subsided, she realized that she was probably still a long way from the path and it was very likely there was no one about to hear her signal. She heard a small sound a little way to her left. She moved over to see what it was and was greeted with a sight that once more sent waves of panic through her. A young rabbit had been caught in a tangle of fine nylon wire, the sort used for fishing. Its efforts to free itself had made matters worse and Helen could see that it had no hope of escape on its own. She turned away, sickened by the sight of this helpless creature. She had to get help for Lucy, she told herself. But who would get help for this rabbit? No other animal could untangle the line. If Helen left it there it would die, but how could she help it? It was hurt. How could she touch it?

She made herself put out her hand towards the little creature, but drew it back quickly as the rabbit flinched away from her. Then she realized that it too was frightened, of *her*. She was the only one who could help it, and it was frightened of her. She spoke in soft, gentle tones and moved her hands more confidently to release it. It seemed an impossible task. She had to hold the little body firmly in order to unwind the mess of line. At last it was done. She stroked the soft fur to calm the little rabbit before setting it on the ground. It scampered off into the bushes as she looked after it, feeling pleased she had accomplished something on her own.

She looked up at the sky. The sun was trying to come out. If she kept it in the same position she must come to a path soon, and that path would lead to another. There was no one to tell her which way to go. She had to make up her own mind. Lucy and Jane were depending on her. One to fetch help, Mrs Morrison had said. Well, she was that one. She couldn't let them down.

She made her way carefully away from the brambles, trying to remember on which side the sun had been as they had walked earlier on. It seemed such a long time ago now. She pulled the map out of her pocket again and decided that she would keep the sun on her left. She wasn't at all certain which direction this would take her in, but she knew she had to decide something or she might just go round and round in circles until...until...She stopped thinking about it as panic began to rise again. She had to stay calm and stick to her plan until she got somewhere.

The way seemed easier to follow now. There were no more brambles and the undergrowth seemed less tangled. The trees were taller with fewer low branches. It didn't look like the woodland that they had followed Lucy into, but the going was easier, so Helen hurried on. She tried to keep the sun on the same side all the time, but it was sometimes hard to see it through the canopy of leaves above. She came to a fallen tree and stopped to have a drink and rest her legs. As she sat there, the silence of the forest was almost oppressive. Then, Helen thought she heard footsteps. Someone was coming through the trees to her right, very quietly, as if they were trying to creep up on her. She felt the hairs on the back of her neck rise and the sweat trickle down her back. She tried to hold her breath. Her heart was pounding so loudly that she was sure whoever it was would be able to hear it.

The quiet noise of walking continued past her and away. She followed the sound with her eyes, growing calmer as the footsteps receded. Then she saw four pricked brown ears and the dappled rumps of two deer, quietly picking their way through the trees. Relief escaped from her lips in a gasp and at the sound, the deer turned. As they saw her they started to run, so lightly that they scarcely made any more noise than before. Then the silence settled once more.

Helen picked up her rucksack and put it on her back. She checked the sun's position and set off again. It was one forty-five and they were due at the meeting place between two and three. No one would be looking for them yet. No one except her and Jane knew that anything had gone wrong. She remembered the ugly bruising on Lucy's temple and wondered how long it would be before anyone arrived to see her.

Suddenly she came out of the darkness of the trees onto a wide path. She unfolded the map once again and turned it this way and that, trying to decide which path she was on. It was no use. She had no idea if she should go left or right. She didn't know why she chose right. It almost seemed to choose itself. She felt absolutely certain that right was the right way to go. She was so certain that she almost ran. The path went slightly uphill and then curved round to the left. It was wide and easy to walk on and Helen made good progress. She began to feel that very soon she would see the others and smell the camp fire and know that she was safe and that help was on its way for Jane and Lucy.

She came to a place where the path forked. Should she go right or left here? Both paths looked equally inviting. She decided on the left one in case she somehow made a complete circle and ended up where she started from. She turned left and almost straightaway the path narrowed and the trees closed in. Thinking that it didn't look very promising she turned back and took the other path. This one also quickly narrowed, but this time she kept going. After a while she was once more ducking branches and trying to avoid brambles. It became hard to see where the actual path was. Reluctantly, she turned back and when she got to the fork she went again up the first path. She was worrying now that she was wasting valuable time, time that might be important for Lucy. She had gone about half a mile up the narrow path before she realized it, too, would not lead her anywhere. It just seemed to disappear. It didn't really stop, it just, suddenly, wasn't there any longer.

Everything was turning into a nightmare. Each path she followed just petered out. Whichever way she went, the path ceased to exist. She could be here all night, following paths that led to nowhere. She imagined the sun going down and her stuck in the forest, unable to find a way out.

She thought of Jane and Lucy, getting colder and colder, relying on her, comforting themselves with the thought that she would bring help for them. But here she was, utterly lost. She fought back the tears she felt pricking the backs of her eyes. 'I'll try the whistle again,' she thought.

She put it to her lips and blew six sharp blasts. She did not imagine this time that anyone would reply. She blew the whistle because she knew the sound of it would comfort her. She put it back in her pocket and had started back down the narrow path when she stopped and turned her head. She could hardly believe her ears! In the distance she heard an answering call. She could scarcely wait until it had finished before she blew her six calls again, stumbling through the trees as she followed the sound. No need to worry if the path disappeared. No need for a path. Follow the sound. Watch the sun. Keep your head. You'll soon be there. You're the one. The one to fetch help.

The sound of the whistle got louder and louder. Helen pounded through the trees, all worries now forgotten. She could hear voices, see flashes of coloured anoraks, smell the campfire. She burst out into the open and tripped over her teacher's feet.

'Helen! Whatever's the matter? Where are the others?'

'Oh! Mrs Morrison. We got lost and Lucy's hurt and I found the way and I've come to fetch help.'

EXCUSES, EXCUSES

KATE HALL

'I have to tell you about Tabitha Tyler, then you'll understand. I'm Nancy Tyler, which is why my cat's called Tabitha Tyler. I don't have any brothers or sisters or a dad. Well, I did have a dad but he died when I was two and I can't remember him very well, so I've got a cat to keep me company. Mum says that we couldn't have a dog because we haven't got a garden and, anyway, they aren't really allowed in the flats. The people downstairs have got one, but my mum says it isn't fair on the dog, without a garden. Anyway, it was all Tabitha Tyler's fault. Well, I suppose some of it was my fault too.

Tabitha Tyler is a very big tabby, with a white front and two white paws at the back. She also has a white bit at the end of her tail, as if she'd dipped it into some paint. She actually did dip her whole self in some paint once, when we were decorating, but that was blue. It took ages to get it off, even with the special stuff that the vet at the RSPCA gave us. We know him quite well and he knows Tabitha quite well because Tabitha Tyler's that kind of cat.

She fell down the chute once and had to be dug out of the rubbish in the big bin at the bottom by the caretaker, who made a terrible fuss. He said if he had his way, all pets would be banned on the estate and that they were more trouble than they were worth. He was even angrier when Tabitha Tyler scratched him, but it really wasn't her fault, she was just very scared. Mum calmed the caretaker down, while I took Tabitha Tyler upstairs to recover from her terrible experience. She smelled horrible and was all sticky. We had to give her a bath, which she did not like at all. I didn't even know you could bathe cats, but Mum said only in very serious emergencies, or when they had so many fleas that powder didn't work and even then a grown-up should do it. Mum needed my help anyway, as Tabitha Tyler is a very big cat and she really did not want a bath at all. When she was wet, she looked much smaller and all bedraggled and upset. She wouldn't let us dry her with the hairdryer, so we rubbed her with a big towel, then I held her by the fire on my lap. I had to hold her because she was determined to get under the settee. In fact, she managed it once and it took us ages to get her out. Mum said she might catch cold if we didn't get her dry.

The people who live next door to us, the Dixons, are quite old. Mum says they're not that old, about the same age as Grandma and Grandad, which seems pretty old to me. Anyway, they're waiting to be rehoused in a ground floor flat, somewhere quieter, they say. Mr Dixon's a bit grumpy sometimes and tells my friend Julie and me to go and play on her balcony downstairs, if we're going to make "all that noise". We don't mind, really, because all the families on Julie's balcony have children and you can make as much noise as you like.

Anyway, Mr and Mrs Dixon have got a budgie and of course, Tabitha Tyler loves that budgie. She sits on their window sill staring at it for hours and hours, unless the Dixons catch her and shoo her away. The budgie looks right back and chirps a lot as if to say, "Can't get me." Which, of course, usually, she can't.

Then today, Mr and Mrs Dixon went out and left their top window open and that's when the trouble began. I was on my way home from school for lunch and as I walked past the Dixons' I glanced in. Mum's always telling me off for being nosey, but it was lucky I did because there, inside Mr and Mrs Dixon's flat, on their table, circling their budgie's cage, was Tabitha Tyler. Her tail was swishing and she was making funny rumbling noises in her throat. The budgie was on its perch, trying to make itself invisible and twittering as loud as it could.

"Tabitha Tyler!" I called "Come here at once."

She stopped and looked at me and then carried on going round the cage, patting at the bars. I called again, but she didn't even look up that time. Sometimes, I think she can understand what I'm saying to her, but just then she didn't even seem to be listening.

I looked at the open window. Maybe if I could get up there, I could just squeeze through, or reach the catch for the bottom one. Maybe I should get Mum, I thought, but I knew that she was already fed up with Tabitha Tyler, mostly because of the six eggs yesterday. I didn't know that cats like eggs. The mess was horrible, so I decided not to call Mum and thought I'd get Tabitha Tyler out on my own. I got hold of the window frame and pulled myself up, but then I slipped down and scuffed the toes of my shoes on the wall. After three goes, I had both feet on the window sill and one arm in the window.

Tabitha Tyler and the budgie stopped quite still and quiet, watching me to see what I would do next. I reached down towards the catch on the window. It had some kind of lock on it and I wasn't sure if it would unscrew like Grandma's, or if you needed a special key like the one we've got. Tabitha Tyler got bored with watching me and started work, clawing and chewing at the cage door.

"No, Tabitha Tyler. DON'T!" I said, not too loud, in case I frightened the budgie even more, or Mum heard me. Then I slipped and there I was, hanging by my jumper which had caught on the window lock, my toes just touching the ground. Just then Mr and Mrs Dixon got out of the lift.

"What on earth are you doing? You thieving, little..." Mr Dixon was lost for words.

Mrs Dixon wasn't though. She started yelling at me to get my arm out of her flat and that she was going to call the police. My mum came rushing out to see what was going on and she started yelling too. I kept trying to explain, but no one was listening to me. More neighbours arrived and everyone was arguing. Then Mrs Dixon pulled my arm and the jumper ripped and I was free. My mum went crazy, telling Mrs Dixon she had no right to go ripping people's clothes and Mrs Dixon said that I had no right having my arm in her window.

Then Mrs Braithwaite, another neighbour, shouted "*Shut up!*" at the top of her voice. I was so surprised, because she's not usually a very noisy person. I think everyone else was surprised too because it all went quiet.

"Maybe, if we ask, Nancy will tell us what has happened here," she said. They all looked at me and I felt very small and a bit scared.

"It's Tabitha Tyler," I said. "She's in your flat, trying to get your budgie."

"A likely story" said Mr Dixon, peering through the window. "I can't see her."

"She was on the table." I said. "I was trying to get her out. She was in there, honestly."

"Well, there's only one way to find out," Mrs Dixon said, getting her key out of her purse.

So we all went into the Dixon's flat. Mrs Dixon searched everywhere, carrying the budgie in its cage, "Just in case," while my mum, Mr Dixon, Mrs Braithwaite and a couple of other neighbours, all looked very hard at me, in my torn jumper. Mrs Dixon came back shaking her head.

"There's no cat anywhere in the flat, so you'd better tell us the truth now, young lady."

My mum got really angry then and said she was sure I wouldn't lie like that and everyone started arguing again. Then, Mrs Braithwaite started to laugh. Everyone stared at her as she put her finger to her lips, 'Shush!' She pointed to the corner where the Dixons kept their rubbish bin.

A small piece of white fur was flicking backwards and forwards, just at one side of the bin. We all stayed very quiet until a nose appeared at the other side. I ran towards

Tabitha Tyler but she was too quick for me and with all of us chasing her, she jumped back out of the window, back into our house and under the settee. By now, everyone was laughing so much, they forgot about me for a minute. My mum put the kettle on and Mrs Dixon put the budgie back in its cage and shut the window.

"Mum, can I have my lunch now?" I asked. "I'm going to be late."

"Go and change your jumper, while I make you a sandwich. And next time, young lady, come and get me."

"Yes, Mum," I said.

"So you see, Mr Baker, that's why I'm back late from lunch. Just think, if the boiler hadn't broken down, so that we couldn't have school dinners, Tabitha Tyler would probably have eaten Mr and Mrs Dixon's budgie."

"Thank you, Nancy. Maybe you could write about it for your story tomorrow."

"Mr Baker, don't you believe me? It's true, honestly. If you weren't new, Mr Baker, you would know all about Tabitha Tyler. I'm always talking about her."

"Nancy, I believe you. No one could possibly make up a story like that."

That's what he thinks.'

TELLING STORIES

TINA KENDALL

For Likka

That night the wind was bursting with sound. Growling like some car revving up in a hurry. Yowling like some cat clambering to be let in from the rain. Clatter, clatter went the glass in the window pane and the trees swished in reply. Lima could just picture the heavy branches swaying solemnly, hardly ruffled at all, while at the extremities, the small leaves would be trembling and quivering, as alive and excited as the shiny goldfish in the bowl downstairs. Shuffling about in her bed, in her little room, Lima could not help feeling the cold.

It was not the brushing of the trees which was stopping Lima from falling asleep. She couldn't doze off that night because she had too much on her mind. The major thing which bothered her was the argument she'd had with her mother just after tea. Lima, her mum and Rachel, along with Joey, her baby brother, had all been sitting round the gas fire, eating toast and jam and listening to some classical music on the radio. It was so peaceful and they were all lounging about, smiling at each other and glowing, feeling warm, when suddenly the doorbell rang.

'I'll go,' said Rachel and got up. She came back in, followed by Tracy and Mandy, two of the girls in her class.

'We've come to find out more about the horse-riding,' said Tracy, looking enquiringly at Lima's mum. Lima felt the blood drain slowly from her face and her stomach made a lurch.

'Oh, crumbs,' she muttered to herself.

'Horse-riding?' Lima's mum said. 'What's all this about horse-riding?'

'Lima says she's going to start horse-riding,' Tracy filled in for her, since Lima was finding it hard to put two words together. Her heart was pounding away so hard, so fast, she thought it might come bursting out of her body.

'It's the first time I've heard anything about horse-riding,' Lima's mum replied, her voice beginning to get that angry ring to it that Lima knew so well...and dreaded.

'She said she was going horse-riding on Saturday afternoon and that it only cost twenty pence for an hour. She said that we could come with her if we wanted to,' Mandy continued.

Lima's mum flicked her eyes across at Lima for a second.

'I'm afraid there's been a mistake, a misunderstanding somewhere,' she said gravely.

Lima stared at her feet, the blood flashing like lightning inside her head.

Eventually, Tracy and Mandy had gone, but gone too was the magic of them all close by the fire, crunching the toast and jam. Lima guessed she was in for it and steeled herself for the onslaught of her mother's anger. There was a moment's silence. A long, heavy silence like a dangling, wet rope, then Lima's mum spoke. It wasn't shouting like Lima expected. It was slow and quiet and controlled.

'Lima, perhaps you'd like to explain to me why you told those girls that lie.'

'I'm sorry, Mum.'

A silence again, while Lima tried to set her face in a sorrowful expression.

'You see, it's just, well, I've been reading all these books on horse-riding. I kept thinking and thinking about how much I wanted to have a go. Then suddenly, I started believing that it was possible, that I was going to start horse-riding lessons. I was so happy, I started telling everyone at school...'

'Well, you're going to look foolish when all your friends find out you were just telling stories.'

'You'd have to travel a good twenty miles just to find a horse round here,' Rachel informed her, drily.

Her mum's words came back to her that night as she listened to the trees and the wind ruffling and shuffling. She was already feeling embarrassed at the prospect of seeing that bunch the next day, wondering if they would go on being friends together, talking to her, playing with her. What worried her even more, was that it was not the first time this sort of incident had occurred.

Just before Christmas last year, Lima had flabbergasted all the kids at school by announcing she was to star as Puss in the annual pantomime. Her friends were full of admiration and respect for a few days. They asked her questions about rehearsals, what it was like to stand there on that brightly lit stage and about the song and dance numbers she was required to do. Lima so excelled herself in coming up with convincing responses that all her friends began asking their parents to book tickets so they could see Lima in action!

During those few days, a mixture of feelings were bobbing up inside Lima. At times she fooled herself into feeling elated, excited at the prospect of her forthcoming theatrical glory. At other times, she felt numb with fear, wondering how on earth she could talk her way out of this situation, or mess, as she sometimes viewed it, and not lose face. Either way, it was very thrilling, which made it all worthwhile.

It was Judith Bradshaw who, not to put too fine a point on it, let the cat out of the bag the following Monday morning.

'We saw the ad for Puss in Boots in the paper and your name's not down, Lima. Someone called Heather Jowett is billed as Puss.'

This called for quick thinking and Lima rose immediately to the occasion. Curious eyes were on her.

'Oh, Heather,' she replied nonchalantly, '...she fell sick at the last minute. I was the understudy to begin with, but now I've got the part.'

It was said firmly, without the slightest hesitation and accompanied by a condescending smile for the benefit of those around her.

'Can I have your autograph, Lima, when you've got the time?' one of the group asked, meekly.

'Let's have another look at one of your song and dance routines, Lima,' someone else ventured.

But Judith Bradshaw was not to be convinced that easily.

'Last minute?' she asked, provocatively. 'I thought the pantomime didn't begin for another two weeks. How can you have stepped in at the last minute?'

'In a manner of speaking,' Lima replied, mysteriously, without so much as a glance at her.

Her heart was fluttering like an agitated bird and the sweat was oozing from around her neck and trickling down her back, but she didn't show her concern. Wrinkling her nose a little and raising her eyebrows with the air of someone who is bored by such goings on, she turned away from the little group and withdrew.

Lying in bed this windy night, Lima chuckled to herself as she thought back to that sticky period. The only solution she had hit upon, not to give the game away, had been to go down with diarrhoea. In fact, it had been so easy to pull the wool over her mum's and Rachel's eyes, that Lima was forced to recognize that she did, in fact, have considerable acting talents. It was simply a question of biding her time, for sooner or later, she was bound to get discovered, her name in neon lights.

Her mysterious illness had lasted ten days. She had always managed to make it to the bathroom when the 'vomiting attacks' came on and to flush the toilet before her mum had time to come and inspect. Once or twice she had actually resorted to putting her fingers down her throat and really making herself sick. A touch of authenticity.

Most of her friends accepted the tale of her sickness with no difficulty and commiserated when, with tears in her eyes, she admitted the doctor had said she was now far too weak to take part in the pantomime.

'Never mind, Lima,' they had said. 'Better luck next time. You'll probably get a part in next year's panto.'

That was how most of them had responded, but Judith Bradshaw and her gang behaved differently.

'Come here puss, puss, puss,' they would taunt her. 'Who's a clever puss then?'

Lima had tried to detach herself as much as possible and ignore them, but one lunch time, while she was in the toilets, she heard the voices of Judith and another girl, Afia.

'If you ask me,' Judith was saying, 'that Lima Rawlins is a proper little good-for-nothing liar. Puss in Boots my foot! I don't believe a word of all that pantomime business. Always telling stories, that one.'

After a while, they had gone back into the playground and Lima, her legs wobbly and her face burning hot, got up. It was hard listening to other people criticize her like that, especially since she had to acknowledge that their criticism was justified.

However, a few moments later, she had returned to her friends in the playground, holding her head firm and high. She might not be a star now, but she was sure that one day fame would cross her path and then, all those jealous onlookers would get their just desserts!

Glowing with thoughts of her illustrious past, as the rain flopped like swatted flies on the window pane, Lima suddenly had an idea. It was, to Lima's mind, a special idea, a golden idea, which seemed to alight like a unique, magnificent butterfly with sparkling, scarlet wings. For a second, it hovered nervously inside Lima's head, as if testing the terrain before posing its delicate wings, but then, satisfied that all was how it should be, it alighted. The idea, which Lima thought was sheer brilliance, was genius, settled and stayed with her.

The idea was simply this: to organise a nationwide, storytelling competition for children in three categories according to age; three to six, seven to ten, and eleven to fourteen. Children all over the country could rack their brains, let their imaginations take running jumps and create some zippy new stories. Fiction, Lima firmly believed, was a darn sight more interesting than reality, which is why, from time to time, she felt compelled to gloss up and embellish her own life with a few dabs of imagination.

It seemed to her that this was a project that could capture the energies of hundreds of children throughout the country; and set hearts and spirits soaring. Lima was virtually bouncing up and down in her bed with excitement. She pushed out of her mind the horse-riding incident and the bother she had got into with her mum. All that seemed a thing of the past. She was already drifting off to distant, exotic horizons and going through a list of things she would be required to do to get her project off the ground when suddenly, unexpectedly, she slumped off to sleep.

It was a very deep sleep indeed; a sleep of contentment and promise, and Lima awoke the next morning, refreshed and renewed and raring to go.

Details of all the things Lima had to do to make her idea materialize would fill pages and actually took her several months to complete. She began by persuading her mum and Rachel that the idea was a marvellous one and, given her track record, that took some doing. When they were finally won over, Lima moved on to tackle friends at school. Some of them were doubtful and sarcastic to begin with and were unable to provide the real help she needed. So, she looked beyond her friends and spoke of the project with her teachers, the headmistress and the local library, who were all full of advice and help. Lima's conviction that this was a good idea that had to be followed through, enabled her to interest other people. She believed she was going to make it happen. Some people she approached tried to put her off by telling her that all children today were capable of doing was watching television, playing video games and eating chips and sweets. Their imaginations had died. Lima set out to prove them wrong.

Her own imagination was burning brightly and she wrote hundreds of letters. It was so thrilling because, even in her writing, she would be presenting herself as someone different. Someone more exciting, stronger and every morning there would be lots of letters in reply.

She rang local companies and radio stations to try and win support. At such times she would experience the pleasure she had known when called upon to do the pantomime song and dance routine. The pleasure of performing.

Several months passed. It was now winter and cold. Lima was feeling a bit fed up one evening when a phone call came. A national children's programme was keen to launch her competition. She was being invited to present details of the competition on the show, in a five minute slot, in three week's time. Lima was going to appear on TV! She was asked to help in the setting up of a jury, organizing sponsors, deciding on a closing date and being involved in the big get together; a televised presentation of the storytelling session.

Her head felt furry and funny after the phone call. The prospect of being on television was exciting in itself, but what was even more wonderful, was the fact that the storytelling contest was going to happen. This was too good to be true. All Lima could do was jump up and down on the settee and for once, neither Rachel nor her mum complained.

When Lima had calmed down, somewhat, and began to think more clearly, she soon realized that, given the mix-ups of the past, it would, probably, be best to say nothing to her friends of her forthcoming TV appearance. It was difficult. It was all so thrilling that it was hard to keep so much happiness and excitement to herself, but Lima had made up her mind to see it through and this time she was going to do it.

She contented herself with walking around with a beaming grin on her face and even burst out laughing from time to time, but she was careful not to breathe a word of her secret to anyone. It was Judith Bradshaw who was among the first to spot the change.

'What's up with Lima? She gets more like a Cheshire cat every day. Maybe someone's asked her to be in the next pantomime! Maybe she's been given a horse of her own,' she scoffed.

Lima paid no heed, remaining calm and cool and detached. Before, she would have told Judith Bradshaw exactly what she thought of her, but this time she just kept on beaming to herself and thinking, 'You're in for a right surprise, you are!' She was sucking on her secret like it was some inexhaustible gobstopper.

Eventually, the great day arrived. Lima had been hopping and flapping like a hen that had just laid a golden egg. Her mum had splashed out on new shoes and a pair of sleek brown cords. She and Rachel had spent hours weaving extension plaits into her hair and had come up with an unusual design that Lima was delighted with. Her life was, all of a sudden, seeming so rosy to her. There was a special sheen of happiness around her face and especially in her eyes. Even so, this did not stop her from feeling nervous.

Lima's legs were weak and wobbly; soft-boiled eggs crossed her mind as she walked with her mum, through the multiple corridors of the television company. When they came to the producer's door, Lima tapped loudly. 'Come in,' said a voice from inside. and in they went.

'Ah, so you're Lima with the bright ideas,' said the producer whose face she was too overcome to take note of.

'Well, let's get straight on down to the studio and show you the ropes.'

Lima's mum stayed behind in the office, while Lima walked by the man's side along more corridors. Finally they turned into a bright airy room. She was introduced to the two presenters who were to help her go through the details of the competition. They seemed friendly enough. Then a strange thing happened. Lima felt as if her head had just sprung a leak; as if it was a bucket full of holes and none of the information that people kept repeating to her would stay put. It kept slithering out straight away. Eventually, Lima was able to recite her lines but the way she spoke sounded wooden and tense. Once, when the camera was pointed at her, she took such a fright that the sequence had to be filmed five times before the director was satisfied. By the time this ordeal was over and done with, Lima was beginning to wish the butterfly with sparkling, scarlet wings had never bothered her in the first place...

After her two hour wait, Lima's mum was relieved to see her daughter, but the look on her face told her all was not well. When she heard that Lima's appearance had left a lot to be desired, she forgot all her promises of a knickerbocker glory on the way home. Lima, feeling glummer than ever, and with no strength left to protest, had to make do with a miserable bus ride home.

More suffering in silence and embarrassment followed as the programme was not going to be transmitted for another two weeks. She was painfully aware that her performance was not worth boasting about. It was a good thing which had gone wrong and she tried to push it far from her mind. Fortunately, one of her friends had given her a guinea pig that same week and all her free time was spent making the animal feel happy and secure and trying, unsuccessfully, to teach her a few tricks.

Then, one day at school, Lima was astonished to see Judith Bradshaw running up to her, all smiles.

'The programme was great last night, Lima, and you were so convincing. Why didn't you tell us about it?'

Suddenly, she remembered. The programme had been broadcast last night and Lima had refused to let anyone put it on, so they had all listened to the reggae show on the radio instead and she had wiped it from her mind.

Judith, with new admiration, was watching her, awaiting her reply. Lima seized her chance and felt her confidence come surging back. Why own up to the fact she had hated every second in the studio? Why tell them all how nervous she had been?

'I'm glad you enjoyed it, Judith,' she replied, magnanimously, and then paused. 'I suppose I kept quiet because I knew that, whatever I said, you'd think I was only telling stories.'

COME STRAIGHT HOME

THELMA PERKINS

'Do you think you could come home from school on your own today, love?'

'Why?' Annie asked.

Annie was surprised. She had never even walked to school on her own. Nor had she ever been allowed to come home on her own. As long as she could remember, her mum or nan had always been around to see her safely there and back. When Annie was seven and had gone up into the Juniors, she had asked her mum if she could go to school with her friends but the answer had always been 'No.'

'I like to know that you get there safely and on time,' her mum had said. 'Besides, you're not old enough.'

'But all my friends walk to school on their own. It's not fair. They'll think I'm a baby.'

It didn't make any difference. After each school holiday when her mum was making sure that her clothes, shoes and everything else still fit her, they would go through the same old rigmarole. Annie would ask if she could go to school with her friends and her mum would always say no.

'Well when will I be old enough to go on my own?' Annie would grumble. 'I'll be at comprehensive school and you'll still be holding my hand!'

'Listen to me, young lady,' her mum would answer, 'just be thankful I care enough about you to organize my life so that I can run you backwards and forwards. I have to be careful what I let you do. You haven't got a dad around and people are quick enough to blame anything that might happen to you on that.'

'Why would people blame anything on me not having a dad?'

She couldn't remember her dad at all. Her mum had once told her that he was 'up north'.

'Where up north?' Annie had asked.

'Manchester,' had been the curt reply.

Annie had persisted. 'If he came from Manchester, why am I black?'

'Because your dad is black. His father was a seaman who settled in Manchester after the war. He came from Somalia and married a woman, your grandmother, who was part Nigerian and part Jewish.'

That was the most her mum had ever told her about her dad. Annie had tried to prolong the conversation, wanting to know where her parents had met and why, if her mum was white, was she black? Had her dad ever seen her? Where was he now? Did her mum have any pictures of him? Her mum had got quite cross and told her to mind her own business, not other people's, and to keep what she knew about herself private.

Annie had shut herself in her room and sulked after that incident. Later, Mum had hugged her and apologized. Then she said that when Annie was older and could understand, she would explain to her about her dad.

When will that be, thought Annie. If her dad was around....

Her mum was always saying things and never giving her straight answers. Annie wished her mum would talk to her more about things like that instead of telling her that she wasn't old enough to understand. Just how old did you have to be to know what was going on around you?

'Are you listening, Annie? You're always nagging me to let you go and come on your own. So now you have the chance. I'll take you to school but then I have to go to the hospital, just for the day. I'll be home by the time you come in, it's just that I might not feel up to coming out to meet you.'

'You never said you were ill, what's wrong with you? Why are you going into hospital? Supposing you...'

'Now Annie, what's wrong with me or why I'm going in doesn't really concern you. Don't worry, I will be here when you come home, I promise.'

Annie laid down her spoon and stood up, pushing her chair away from the table. It was always the same, never telling her what was going on as if she was stupid or something. Suddenly she didn't want to come home on her own any more. Nan couldn't meet her. Since she had retired she had moved to be near her Auntie June. There wasn't anyone else. Supposing her mum didn't come out of the hospital. What would happen to her if there wasn't anyone to let her in?

Annie was quiet and worried on the walk to school. The October sun shone weakly through the grey sky and heavy clouds were gathering, threatening rain before the day was through. There was that smell of wet leaves and smoke that always seemed to accompany autumn. Annie's mind was in a turmoil. She hadn't really been listening to what her mum was saying. All she really wanted was for her mum to be at the gate when she came out of school.

'Don't hang about, cross on the crossing, don't go off to your friend's house and don't talk to anyone. Don't take a lift from anyone, not even if you know them. Are you listening to me, Annie?'

'Yes, Mum.'

'Okay then, give me a kiss, have a good day and come straight home now, mind.'

Now that she was just past her tenth birthday, Annie had only one more year at her junior school. She liked school and enjoyed the company of her friends, children she had known from her nursery school days. She rarely went to their homes because, for some reason, her mum hardly ever let her. However, she was allowed to bring friends to her home after school and her mum would let one or two of them accompany them on an outing during the holidays or at weekends.

Today it would have been just great if Mum had let her bring someone home. Clare and Sue were in the school football team and tonight was practice night so they couldn't have come anyway. If it had been swimming club then one of the other mums would have dropped her home and would have seen her safely inside the door. Annie loved swimming. Next to reading it was her favourite hobby. Her shelves at home were weighed down with books. At the moment she enjoyed reading anything spooky and scary. Her teacher had said that it was very evident in the writing she did at school. Her mum said she was surprised she could sleep as soundly as she did!

Annie couldn't even concentrate on reading at school that day. All day long she thought about her mum at the hospital. What was wrong with her? There had to be something wrong or else she wouldn't have had to go in. Supposing she died, how would Nan or Auntie June know? What would happen to her? Why didn't Mum tell her things? She was always talking to her. She even answered her questions, but she never really told her anything. And now she was in the hospital. Which hospital? And there was another thing. Why was Mum always telling her not to tell other people her business? She said that some people managed to get the wrong end of the stick about anything, and that gossip was often the cause of people falling out with family, losing friends and falling foul of the authorities. The less people knew about their personal lives, the better. Mum was always telling her that, so she couldn't even let on about her being ill.

The day seemed to drag by slowly. Annie got into trouble for not paying attention. She didn't feel like doing anything in the playground with her friends and could hardly eat her lunch. Most of all, she wasn't looking forward to walking home on her own in the autumn dusk.

'Please be there Mum, at the gate,' she kept saying to herself.

She was still saying it as she went to collect her coat from the cloakroom. She said it as she silently put it on and buttoned it up. The words rolled around inside her head as she followed the other children across the hall and out into the grey drizzle that was falling. She almost said it out aloud as she crossed the playground and reached the gate.

'Bye, Annie,' her friends called. 'See you tomorrow.'

Annie desperately wished one of her friends would invite her home, even though her mum had warned her against it that morning. None of the other children waited to see if her mum was there. They were all so used to Annie greeting her as she waved goodbye to them; used to seeing the two of them walking hand in hand towards the cemetery that was so close to her home.

Annie looked up. Her mum wasn't there. She felt her stomach drop. She looked up and down the road just in case she was a bit late, but no, her mum wasn't there.

Annie put her hands in her pockets and turned into the drizzle. She began to plod along the road. At the traffic lights she pressed the button and waited for the green man to appear. As the beeps started she crossed quickly, scurrying a little as the wind blew leaves and litter across her path. Along the road Annie passed the newsagents and the chip shop. If I had known Mum wasn't well, I could have bought us some chips for tea, she thought, as the smell drifted out. If Mum wasn't well...she might not even be there...oh what would she do if she couldn't get in?

Annie turned the corner into her road, shivering slightly. Her mind was now wracked with terrible thoughts. The road was long and it curved round in an 's' bend. There were houses only on one side. On the other side was the cemetery bounded by high iron railings. Tall trees, almost bare of leaves, swayed and creaked in the wind. Leaves and litter skittered along, swirling up and then down again as the wind rose and fell. Mum had always said how much she loved autumn, the leaves changing colour, the smell of the damp earth, the late October sunshine and the sort of foods that meant autumn. Annie had agreed with her about them; baked potatoes, hot chocolate, steamed treacle pudding! Dark evenings were fine when Mum was there to hurry you along and give you clues about what was for tea. But now the wind was cold, the drizzle was miserable and gathering gloom was scary.

Annie stopped quite suddenly. She had heard a sound. All thoughts of her mum and the empty house left her mind as she strained to hear the sound again. The wind stopped too. Annie began to walk carefully and quietly. The wind blew, phlat...phlat...phlat...phlat. It sounded as if someone was walking behind her. Should she stop? Should she turn around? Annie began to walk faster. The wind blew again. Phlat...phlat...phlat...phlat. The long shadows cast from the street lamps seemed to be moving with her. It hadn't been this dark when she and Mum had walked home yesterday. Phlat...phlat. An empty crisp bag flew past and the trees on the other side of the road swayed and creaked. Phlat...phlat...phlat...phlat. Annie's feet went faster and faster and so did her heart. It seemed that the faster she walked, the faster the steps were behind her. Getting wet didn't matter now. The cold wind blowing made no difference, all she could hear was the noise behind her. Phlat...phlat...phlat...phlat...phlat...phlat.

The wind tugged at her coat collar and whipped leaves past her face. Annie pulled her hands from her pockets and began to run. All her earlier thoughts about the season were gone from her head as her mum's voice echoed: 'Come straight home, come straight home.' Someone was following her. There was no doubt about that, but her mum's words were law. She didn't dare stop to knock at anyone's door. All she could hear was the slapping noise of feet as they seemed to get faster and closer. She was nearly home when another thought flashed through her mind. What if Mum isn't there? The thought almost made her stop.

There was a roaring in her ears, so loud it almost drowned the noise behind her. The wind died for a few seconds and Annie slowed down. As she did so, so did the noise.

'Come straight home.'

Annie speeded up as the wind rose. As it rose the footsteps started up again. Annie began to run. The noise got faster. Now her feet scarcely touched the ground. She was nearly there.

'Please be there Mum.'

Her wet hands fumbled at the gate. The wind was roaring, but above it she could hear the noise getting closer. Her breath burned in her throat. She struggled to press down the catch. Just as she was about to scream the gate gave way. She fell through.

The noise went past as Annie stumbled onto the path. For a moment she stopped and turned her head round. Her legs felt weak and she began to shake, no, not with terror, but with relief. Past the gate and on down the road went a large piece of corrugated cardboard, caught by the wind. The noise that it had made each time it hit the ground was just like the sound of a foot hitting the wet pavement. When the wind dropped, the cardboard stopped. When the wind whooshed and eddied, the cardboard carried on its journey, flapping and slapping along the pavement.

'It's a bit like the stories I read,' Annie thought, as she reached out weakly to ring the bell.

The door opened.

'Hello, love, you all right, managed it on your own then? Have you been running? You're all out of breath.'

'Yes, Mum, no problem. I ran because it was wet and windy. Are you okay? I came straight home just like you said.'

Her mum reached out and drew her inside. Giving Annie a hug and a kiss she said, 'Guess what's for tea?'

L O I S

TERESA SAVAGE

Lois was a smart girl. No one said she was a pretty girl, but Lois didn't care. She liked to wear her brother's old football boots, jodhpurs, and an old flat cap her dad used to wear on the docks. Although her mum thought it was sensible for her to wear those kinds of clothes for playing in, whenever it was time to go out she'd say; 'Come on Lois, let's get you looking pretty', but Lois still wore the flat cap.

One day Lois's mum said they had to go meet her auntie, who'd been in Australia for years and years; an aunt Lois had never seen before. Laid out on the bed for her to wear was a new dress with frills all around the neck that itched, and on the floor were a pair of little white shoes that pinched her toes when she tried them on.

'Make sure you leave that cap at home, Lois,' her mother shouted up the stairs but while Mum was packing the bags in the car, Lois got an old carrier bag and threw in her cap and jeans and a pair of wellie boots.

'Just in case,' she told herself, and sneaked them into the back of the car, under her feet.

'What's she like then, Auntie Madeline? Why's she been in Australia?'

'Oh, she went to live there with her friend Stella; she's Australian.'

'Yes, but what's she like?'

'I expect she's changed a lot. She was my baby sister. I used to call her Matty and she would follow me everywhere.

She looks like me too, but she always knew her own mind. Anyway, we'll see her soon enough.'

Lois's mum steered the car off the motorway and into the airport. As they parked the car, Lois stuffed her old teddy into the top of the carrier bag and off they went, following the signs for 'Arrivals.'

'What have you got in that bag, Lois?'

'Oh just some toys in case I get bored waiting.'

It was a long wait. The plane from Sydney had been delayed, so they just sat there with all the other people, just waiting. There was a man stretched out asleep on the floor beside her and people with cameras and huge trolleys full of luggage trundling past. Lois felt more and more uncomfortable. Her toes were squashed in her new white shoes and her neck was red and sore from all her scratching.

'Stop fidgeting, Lois,' said Mum, while Lois noticed that her mum had kicked off her shoes and was stretching out her toes. Nearby was a ladies toilet and after half an hour, Lois told her mum that she needed to go.

'Okay,' she said, 'but hurry, I think Aunt Madeline will soon be coming through.'

Five minutes later, Lois came out of the Ladies. She stood there dressed in her jumper, old jeans and wellies and on her head was her dad's old cap. The frilly dress and shoes had been stuffed in the carrier bag.

When Lois's mother saw her, her mouth fell open. Just as she was about to give Lois a big telling off, someone behind her said,

'Oh, I'm so glad you could come to meet us.'

Lois looked up to see her Aunt Madeline and Stella, staggering up to them with a trolley load of luggage. Aunt Madeline was wearing tough leather boots, jeans, a check shirt, and on her head was an old flat cap.

'Er...hello,' said Mum, as she gave Aunt Madeline a big hug.

'And this must be Lois!', said Aunt Madeline. 'G'day Lois, I've been wanting to meet you for a very long time.'

THE GREAT ESCAPE

ZEINA CARRINGTON

Were we really going to do it? Or would I lose my courage? How could I lose my courage now? Everyone knew what we intended to do. If I failed now, or at least failed to attempt to do it, I would lose my credibility; I would lose my standing in the secret detective club I had invented myself. I shuddered in my bed, oh Lord, how had I got myself into this predicament? Well, of course, it had all started with the coming of Marianne.

Marianne came to the children's home in Rosemary Road as a last resort. Her speciality was running away. Her reputation had gone before her. She had run away from every children's home we knew of just as she had run away from her own home many years before. It was never clear why she had run away in the first place but I understood completely why she had run away from all the other children's homes. They were no place for a child to grow up. Certainly here at Rosemary Road, it felt more like a children's prison and not the kindly reception home it was made out to be. Rosemary Road was a place where the authorities brought confused children whose home situations had broken down somehow; either because of divorce or abandonment, or sometimes because of the death of a parent.

Here at the home, everything was organized along military lines. We all had names but numbers were used to make things easier for the 'aunties' and 'uncles' who worked here. I was number five. My number could be found inscribed on everything that had anything to do with me: my brush, my flannel, my towel, my clothes. It was a wonder they never thought to tattoo it on our arms! The aunties and uncles only called us by our names if they were trying to be particularly caring, and even then it was usually your surname. '...Carrington!!' they would shout. That was me.

Marianne had arrived that afternoon but by the evening she had had enough. She was planning to run away, and to my amazement, she had honoured me by asking me to go with her. Before she had arrived I had been the leader of our little gang, but her credentials were far greater than mine. If I didn't go with her I knew I would lose the respect of the others. Anyway, it was a good idea. Who wanted to stay here anyway? It was just that I had never really considered escape as an option. But why not? Here was my chance and we had a real expert to lead us.

Everything had been planned for my sister and her friend Jane to come with us. All we had to do was wait until deepest night and then we would put the plan into action. The basic idea was that we were to get ourselves onto a train heading for Hampshire, back to the countryside and the wonderful place my sister and I had lived before with our caring and loving foster mother. Of course the plan involved a certain amount of dishonesty, since we had no money whatsoever to pay for our train ticket, but Marianne said she knew how it could be done.

At about two o'clock in the morning, when all was quiet, I felt someone shaking my shoulder. I woke up to find Marianne's face peering down at me.

'Come on, it's time,' she said.

'What, now?' I glared, astonished.

'Yes, hurry, or we won't have time,' she said urgently.

'What shall I do?' I asked, terrified and shaking, as I realized that it was really on. This was for real.

'The plan of course,' she replied reproachfully.

I jumped out of bed and swung into action. I woke my sister and told her to wake Jane. I then gave her two plastic bags and a vanity case and told her to pack essential warm clothes. I took the case from my petite typewriter and began to stuff it with clothes from my drawer, not worrying whether they matched. I put on my dressing gown and slippers, placed my pillow under the bedclothes, to make it look as if I was still there, and tiptoed over to the others with two full bags of clothes. We all gathered at the top of the stairs, half giggling and half shaking in disbelief. Blurry eyed we descended to the large kitchen, opened the immense wardrobe-sized fridge freezer and packed our bags to the brim with all the goodies we had never been allowed to eat because it was 'staff food.' Lovely ripe grapefruits, little pots of fruity yoghurts and two loaves of bread.

'Come on,' urged Marianne, impatiently.

'All ready?' I asked the two little ones. My sister and Jane nodded excitedly as if we were going on a magical mystery tour.

For a moment I stopped feeling petrified as we giggled quietly, running out of the back door on our tip toes with our bags full to the brim, dressed in slippers, pyjamas and dressing gowns. As we slipped out of the door I caught sight of our anoraks and wellington boots, which I called my welligogs, and quickly threw off my dressing gown and slippers and changed into them. Much more practical for running away, I thought. My sister and Jane couldn't find theirs, in spite of the number system. Marianne changed into her shoes because as a new arrival she had no boots as yet.

At last we were out into the night, running down the quiet suburban street. Not a soul stirred, not a bird sang, and apart from the streetlights, there wasn't a single light on anywhere. The night was like our mantle, our protection on the road to freedom. My lungs felt as if they had doubled in size as I breathed in the air that I romantically believed carried the smell of everything that was fresh and innocent. I wasn't quite sure where we were running to and looked towards Marianne.

'Where to?'

'To the station of course!'

'Oh,' I said, grabbing my sister's hand so that she wouldn't fall behind.

'You know the way, don't you?' asked Marianne crossly.

'Of course,' I said.

'I do!' offered my sister.

'And I do,' echoed Jane.

To them it was an outing, a bit of fun. It dawned on me that they probably didn't really realize the seriousness of this venture. Well, I hardly realized it myself, to tell the truth. We had reached a small clump of trees on the opposite side of the road from the small country station we were heading for.

'Let's change our clothes here,' I said.

'Good idea,' said Marianne, approvingly.

We rested a while and changed out of our night clothes. It was at this point that our first mistake became obvious. I had a full set of clothes, more or less, and the protection of an anorak and my welligogs. Marianne likewise. My sister and Jane, however, had no underpants and no shoes. Well, at least they had thick woolly tights but what would people say when they saw the two little ones in slippers? I realized that I would have to be ready with a credible explanation in case anyone should ask. We decided to keep the two little ones' dressing gowns because they were made of heavy wool and would be good for keeping them warm at night; but no matter how hard we tried we could not repack all our night clothes in our bursting bags.

'We'll have to leave them here,' said Marianne, decidedly.

'Yes of course,' I said, as I proceeded to hang them up in the trees. I didn't really want to leave them on the muddy ground, my pyjamas were quite new after all!

'All ready?' asked Marianne.

'Yes,' I said, as I hurriedly finished dressing my sister and Jane.

Maybe it had been a mistake bringing them along. Marianne did not seem to realize that they were three years younger and therefore needed a little patience and assistance. It had run through my mind several times to turn back and forget the whole thing, but the idea of facing the penalties that I was sure we would get, kept me going. We had already gone too far. There was no turning back now.

'Right, it's to the station then, and then it's up to you to get us on without a ticket,' I said to Marianne, trying to sound my most commanding.

'It's easy,' she retorted, 'come on!'

We crossed the road and ran down the little path which was really the second entrance to the station. It was beginning to get light. It must be around three or four in the morning, I thought. There was no one in the little sentry box. Thank God, I thought. There couldn't have been many people to collect tickets from at that time in the morning.

'There's never anyone guarding exits at this hour,' said Marianne, as if she had read my mind.

Well there could have been, Miss Clever Clogs, I thought to myself. How was she to know!

Once on the other side of the little swing gate, we sat and waited for the train, hidden by the sentry box from the one other person who was also waiting for an early morning train.

'That's good,' I said.

'What?' asked my sister.

'There's someone waiting; it means there should be a train soon,' I explained.

'Of course there's a train coming, there always is,' said Marianne, arrogantly throwing back her black hair. Marianne made me cross when she tried to make us feel small in that way.

'Well, I suppose you should know, you've done it enough times, haven't you?' I said.

I felt a bit nervous. I knew I would feel better once we were safely on the train. A nice, fast train taking us away from here. How I longed to see Winnie again, my kind wonderful foster mum. She had cared for us before we had fallen back into the hands of the numerous aunties and uncles who treated us like numbers on a piece of paper. Surely all this was worth it; putting up with Marianne, whose expertise I depended on so much. Once we arrived at Winnie's, everything would be all right again. Surely she would never let us go now, not once we had explained to her how unhappy we all were.

Suddenly, miracle of miracles, a train! Oh, but such a short one. Once the other person had got on we ran for our lives, dived in and slammed the door shut, safe! Our bodies were quivering all over as we giggled in disbelief. Even Marianne seemed surprised that we had pulled it off. A yoghurt tumbled out of one of the stuffed bags and we all dived onto it laughing, our eyes streaming with tears of relief. We had no spoon of course, so we all passed it round, drinking and licking our way through it.

'Another one?' I said.

'Yes!' we all agreed. It was good that we all agreed, I thought, but there was bound to come a time when we might not and then what would we do?

'Right, we have to make some rules,' I said urgently.

'Rules! What rules?' said Marianne.

'Rules, like we have in our detective club,' explained my sister in a matter of fact way. I smiled. Sisters can be useful sometimes. One thing I was good at was organizing, just as I had done in our secret club in the children's home. I proposed that we should stick together, whatever happened, and that nothing would be decided on unless we all agreed. If really necessary we would even have to go to a vote.

'Agreed?' I asked.

'Yes,' replied a chorus of voices.

Immediately I felt at ease. This way Marianne couldn't abandon us, or make us do anything we didn't want to.

Anyway, the two little ones knew me better. I guessed they would probably be on my side if it came to a showdown.

We settled in comfortably and took to watching out of the window as we sped away from our misery.

'Number five, time to get up,' I shouted.

'Time to clean the shoes,' said my sister.

'Time to wash the dishes,' screamed Jane in delight.

'Time to go to bed,' I said.

'Time to be punished!' said Marianne, looking out of the window. 'That's how we live, like prisoners, like criminals, that's why I never stay in those homes. They're nice to you at first and then when you're fooled, they put the boot in.'

I felt sad for Marianne all of a sudden. I understood her feelings totally but I had never had the courage to be openly defiant. My heart warmed to her as I bent forward and held her hand.

'We would never have made it without you,' I said. We hugged warmly. Everything was going to be all right. I felt aglow inside. Jane was about to eat the third yoghurt.

'No,' I said. 'We must save some for later.'

'How are we going to buy food without any money?' asked my sister.

'We're going to do bob-a-jobs,' I said.

'And we can always pick flowers and sell them door-to-door. Especially daffodils. There's always loads in the park,' said Marianne.

'But we shouldn't pick the flowers in the parks, should we?' I asked.

'It doesn't say anywhere that we shouldn't,' said Marianne. 'I've done it before and no one said anything.'

'Oh,' I replied, perplexed. I shrugged my shoulders in resignation. These were desperate times, we could be forgiven just this once for doing wrong.

'I think we should get off here,' said Marianne.

'Why here?' I said. 'There are too many people.'

'There's only three or four,' said Marianne. But it was too late. The train had pulled away.

'The next one, definitely,' said Marianne.

I looked at the two little ones. They were ready with their bags, ready to leap off just as they had leapt on. We were all ready. At the next stop we went for it. We leapt off and ran. All this was hardly necessary since, once again, there appeared to be no ticket collector. So where were we? Holmwood, I read. I wondered how far that was from Odiham in Hampshire where Winnie's house was.

'I wish I'd brought a map,' I said aloud. I decided that a map would be one of the first things we bought once we'd earned our first bob-a-job money. How could we possibly think of getting anywhere without a map!

Once out on the street we had two options; to turn left towards what looked like the little village centre, or right, to who knows where. We decided to go to 'who knows where' and after five minutes of walking, as if out of a story book, we came upon a little expanse of muddy water on the edge of a woodland area which seemed to disappear eventually, into rampant fields. Perfect! That's where we would make our home, our camp, our hideout.

'I want to feed the ducks,' said Jane,

'We've got plenty of bread,' I said, as I dived into the food bag and pulled out a loaf. We split the loaf and sat ourselves down in the mud, throwing our morsels to the delighted, congregating ducks. What time was it, I wondered. Then I thought, 'who cares?' I decided that it was probably about eight o'clock.

'They'll be getting up by now,' I said victoriously.

Marianne laughed. 'Yeah!' she said, smirking. She had won again. She had preserved her reputation. No place could hold her, she was a free spirit. I caught her eye again and sent her a message of warmth.

'We must build a camp,' said my sister.

The loaf was finished, so we set to work, looking for broken bits of trees and strong sticks to use as uprights.

'Look, over here,' said Jane.

We ran to where she was, a little further into the woods.

'What amazing luck,' I said, as I saw a seriously constructed camp, lined with bright coloured pieces of plastic and furnished with two old car seats.

'I wonder who it belongs to?' I said. 'Maybe they'll come back and catch us if we use it.'

'Well, we can stay here for now and then build another one later,' said Marianne. 'We can store our bags here.'

We clambered into the shelter and tried out the seats. I pulled out a grapefruit.

'Want some?' I asked around.

We sat peeling two of the four grapefruits, laughing and playing camps, choosing where we would sleep and store our belongings, and then just generally messing around, in fun. I noticed the little ones' slippers were now totally clogged and soggy with mud. Their thick tights were already torn and their little feet were wet and cold and already scratched from running around in the prickly woodlands. I felt guilty because my feet were warm and dry in my welligogs. Quietly I hoped they wouldn't catch cold. I added socks and boots to my mental list of things to buy as soon as possible, along with the map. After a while Marianne started to get agitated and restless.

'Let's go walkabout,' she suggested. 'We should have a good exploration of this area so that we know where we really are.'

We all stood up. I was worried about the little ones' feet.

'We'll be all right,' said my sister. I suggested we stick to the paths and so avoid unnecessary prickles and stings, so their feet might not get cut any further.

We set off to survey our new kingdom. We followed paths, crossed streams, and scrambled across fields. We decided to use the local railway track as our guide so that in the event of any of us getting lost we could more or less follow it back to the camp.

It was like being born again. The little ones forgot the pain in their feet, and I forgot to worry about them. I don't know where we found the energy, but there was plenty of it. Even doing little things made us feel excited, like climbing trees, picking and gorging ourselves on berries, rolling around in the tall grass and searching for four-leaved clovers. Wondering what they would they be doing at home. Playing the numbers game I shouldn't wonder, military style! I decided that children's homes were a sin. I lay on my back in the grass with the others, lazily glancing up at the spring sun, a piece of tall grass turning in my mouth. I wouldn't have missed this for the world.

We ate the last loaf of bread and shared out the last two grapefruits. There was no more food. Even though we were hungry we were still happy as we made our way back to camp. Our anoraks and jumpers were now ripped and torn and the little ones' feet were a mess of thorny cuts and stings. I ended up carrying my little sister for the last stretch on my back. It was now late afternoon. The breeze was stronger and the sun's heat weaker. We rested in the camp after washing their feet in the muddy pond and then wrapped them up in their dressing gowns.

'I'm hungry,' bleated my sister.

'So am I,' sobbed Jane.

Oh here we go, I thought. Now would come the whining and complaining amid the tears. Marianne and I gently tried to explain that running away was not all fun, that there was a purpose to it, that we were going to see Winnie and then everything would be all right.

'But when, when!' whined my sister, like only she knew how.

'Tomorrow,' I said firmly. 'Tomorrow we'll get the train to Winnie's, won't we?' I looked hard at Marianne, searching for support.

'Sure, yeah,' assured Marianne. 'We'll go off now and get some food. You two should stay here, snuggle down and rest, okay?' she said cuddling Jane while I cuddled my sister.

We would have to care for them.

Once we were out of the den I turned to Marianne and asked, 'How will we get food with no money?'

'How d'ya think?' she said, giving me a look that made me feel like a complete idiot.

'What...you mean steal it!' I said, open mouthed and shocked. I had never shoplifted anything in all my life. I knew I couldn't do it,

'I can't...I...I...I just can't do it Marianne. I'll just end up getting us both arrested!'

'Don't worry,' she said. 'I'll do it, you just wander around casually being normal. We have to do it. The little ones need something to eat, there's nothing else we can do. If we ask someone or knock on someone's door, they're sure to get suspicious and call the police. I've been caught like that before.'

Well it all seemed logical enough, maybe we could get away with it just this once. We waved goodbye to the little ones and then went off foraging. We walked two miles up the road after deciding not to go back into the town for fear of being spotted. This wasn't going to be easy, I thought. No big supermarkets here. Holmwood was good for woodland camps but it was no shopping city. My plastic bag was ready, stuffed into my torn anorak pocket. I was hoping we could bring it back stuffed full of goodies so that the little ones wouldn't cry again. Finally we came upon a small corner shop. We strolled in trying to look casual. I was sure I had 'GUILTY' written in red across my forehead. I browsed around trying to look thoughtful. I dared not look at Marianne. After about five minutes, Marianne left the shop and I swiftly followed.

'Well?' I asked urgently.

'Well nothing, it was impossible. It's too small, the shop. All I got was this!'

Marianne put her hand in her pocket and pulled out a raspberry ice-lolly.

'What good is that?' I screamed in horror. 'That's no good to anyone. We need food, proper food. You're hopeless. I thought you could do this sort of thing. You haven't the nerve have you? You're not the hot shot you think you are!' I ranted and raved in exasperation amid streaming tears of frustration. I was tired. It wasn't fun any more. Nothing was working out. I was hungry, I was sore and I felt weak.

'I'm going back to camp,' I said as I marched off, not even checking to see if Marianne was following. How was I going to explain our failure to the little ones? I felt totally at a loss.

By the time we arrived back at the camp, the light was rapidly fading. All I wanted to do was lie down, close my eyes and sleep. Tomorrow I would sort out the problems. Tonight I would sleep. I approached the entrance of the den in anticipation of rest.

'Marianne! Marianne! Come quickly.'

A mixture of nausea and anxiety rose from the pit of my stomach. The den was empty. The two little ones were nowhere to be seen. Even more remarkable was that their bags were gone too.

Marianne ran up to the scene of the crisis.

'Oh they must have gone home,' she said.

'Oh shut up,' I said in tears. 'You know they wouldn't do that.'

'What then? Do you think someone's taken them...like the police...or someone else?'

I could feel the horror thundering in my head like a waking nightmare.

'A bogey man. The bogey man has carried off the little ones.'

Oh no! We would find their little bodies in the undergrowth, or floating in the duck pond. Immediately we started running around in circles, screaming their names with all the power and urgency we could muster.

'J..A..N..E..!!'

Then a silence to hear a possible response. Nothing.

'T..O..O..T..S!!'

Still nothing. We shouted their names again and again, but there was not a sound, not a sign. We were done for. We had lost the little ones. I feared I would never see my sister again.

I cried and wailed bitterly, burying my anguished face in the rough bark of a tree I had chosen to embrace in my desperation. I howled and screamed in torrents of tears, like a dying wolf. Would this nightmare ever be over, or would we be damned for all eternity?

Marianne looked on in silence, for once having no explanations, forlorn and pale, looking off into the distance. For a moment her eyes fixed on something across the road at the edge of the woods. I followed her narrowing gaze.

'What? What is it?' I asked.

'Someone's coming towards us,' she said. 'Quick, let's run.'

'No!' I said, 'Maybe they've got the little ones.'

I could see the figure of a man approaching the edge of our kingdom. As he drew nearer, I could see more clearly that he was dressed in a uniform...a police uniform! I turned towards Marianne and, without a word, but with one accord, we ran to the den to gather our belongings. We stuffed all our things in a frenzied muddle into the bags and started backing out of the den, ready to launch into full flight. Then I felt it. I felt it firmly on my shoulder; the classic, firm grip of the arm of the law, stopping me in mid flight.

"Ello 'ello, and where do you think you're going to? On holiday are we then?' came the sarcastic tone.

I turned, saw his face and I knew, at that moment, that it was all over.

The relief did not really come until we were bundled into a waiting police car, for inside sat my sister and Jane, drinking fruit juice and eating chocolate bars. Pleased as punch, my sister's impish eyes lit up.

'Hello, we've been waiting for you. We've told the police everything...you see we got fed up and Jane and I decided we wanted to go home. It was fun though...while it lasted, you know...running away and all that.'

I looked at my sister in disbelief, as I registered her betrayal, remembering how I had cried for her, and all this time she had been safe and eating chocolate!

I looked out across the edge of the woods. If I took my chance now I could make a dash for it. A last flame of desire sparked and went out as I contemplated the idea and then decided against it. The car pulled away as I sat quietly crying inside, as I realized that with each mile we were leaving paradise and nearing certain punishment and retribution. What would they do to us? Lock us up! No pocket money for a thousand years. Number five to clean shoes forever, clean the floors, scrub the potatoes, shine their personal silver. Surely the sentence would be forever.

On the other hand there was glory. We had done it...really done it. We had dared to escape, even though it had only lasted one day, it would be remembered forever. I would become like Marianne, my reputation would go before me. I would be labelled 'difficult', a 'bad influence', a 'management problem'.

'I don't care,' I sniffed to myself. 'It was worth it.'

It was worth it for one day of freedom; one day to go where I pleased, to eat when I pleased and breathe when I pleased. I could see the sun setting in flames on the horizon as I solemnly promised myself to keep the memory of this day alive and never to have any regrets. I knew that if I was clever, I could live off the memory of this one day of freedom when the difficult times ahead got me down. I would remember with an inward grin, the day we outsmarted all of them and commandeered *the great escape!!*

THE COMPETITION

ANNE HALL

The problem with having the same name as someone else is that it encourages comparisons, and Pat Baker and I were completely different. I was big for my age; she was small. I had straight, mousey, fair hair and she had shiny, black curls. I wasn't pretty, she definitely was. I'd never had a boyfriend, boys were always hanging around Pat. If she'd had a pound for each time her initials had been scrawled on the walls of our school playground, she would have been rich enough to pay for our dream to go to Hollywood together. In spite of our differences at the age of ten, we shared the ambition to become film stars. In fact, we had already started saving the fare in a box we kept in Pat's bedroom. I wasn't too happy about the money being at Pat's house, since I didn't trust her older sister, Maureen, who had recently started smoking and always seemed to be on the scrounge. She'd been at work for three months but spent all of her wages on clothes and make-up.

'My money-box has a key, yours hasn't,' Pat said, with the authority of a city banker, so that was that.

There was no doubt that Pat was the natural leader in our friendship. She wasn't bossy. I wouldn't have stood for bossiness. I was no doormat, even if I was shy. It was more a question of courage and I always felt that she knew more than I did. Not in the way that someone cleverer knew more, in fact Pat didn't do as well at school as I did, but in the way that someone older knows more. Both Pat's parents worked so Pat was on her own a lot in the school holidays.

She was expected to clean the house, do the shopping and peel the potatoes for tea every day.

'If you can do Mrs Baker's housework, you can do mine,' Mum protested each time I said I was going to go round to call for Pat. Mum knew from Mrs Baker's proud boasts how much housework she made Pat do.

'I shan't do any,' I lied. 'I shall just wait for Pat to finish, then we'll go to the park.'

It was a bit dodgy telling lies to Mum, since Pat only lived next door, but I supposed that we might go to the park. I did feel a bit guilty helping Pat with the cleaning, I must admit, especially as I couldn't stand Mrs Baker and really I was very fond of Mum. I also knew that Mum hated housework as much as I did. But, it was so different round at Pat's. We had the house to ourselves. We were in charge. We could eat when we wanted and what we wanted, within reason. We could play the record player louder than we wanted. It was like playing at house but with the real thing, with the whole thing, not with just a corner of the kitchen or your bedroom. A bit of housework was such a small price to pay for the pleasure of playing grown-ups for a few hours.

However, I must admit, that wasn't all there was to it. If it had been, I expect the novelty would soon have worn off. No, what really drew me to Pat's house day after day was what we did upstairs. In our street, the upstairs of every house was sacrosanct. You were welcomed into the kitchen, admitted into the living-room, tolerated on special occasions such as birthdays and Christmas in the front room but always, no matter what the circumstances, forbidden the bedroom. Once, I had dared to wait for Pat at the bottom of their stairs, while she fetched something from her bedroom. Mrs Baker had announced quietly and mysteriously:

'I think you had better wait in the kitchen, Pat. Mr Baker's using the bathroom.'

Even my own mother, who was more lax about having kids in the house than most, was reluctant to have them upstairs, but I had always assumed that she was a [...] ashamed about us having no carpets on the bedroom floors, as I was. I was no longer sure that was the reason. There was something forbidding and secretive about the upper floor of other people's houses and possibly my own.

I held my breath and trembled on every tread when Pat led me up their stairs for the very first time. I think that I was half afraid of being suddenly trapped by Mr Baker leaping from the bathroom, half-clothed and indignant to bar my passage at the top of the stairs and Mrs Baker, fully clothed and furious, blocking my exit at the bottom.

I relaxed a little when Pat took me into her own room and we became absorbed in the guided tour she gave through her drawers and cupboards. Pat tired of this much sooner than I did.

'I bet you'd like to see our Maureen's things, wouldn't you?' she asked suddenly and without waiting for a reply, she closed the dressing table drawer we were examining, smoothed the creases on the counterpane where we'd been sitting and pulled me through the door and across the landing.

'Our Maureen'd kill me if she could see us now,' she giggled as she flung open Maureen's fitted wardrobe door. My fear returned as I was about to make up some excuse about having to go home when Pat pushed a pair of the loveliest shoes I had ever seen at my chest.

'Here, try these on. I bet you're the same size as our Maureen. They're like boats on me.'

The fear of being caught, and the embarrassment of having the same size feet as someone who had been at work for three months, were easily overcome by the desire to try on the gorgeous pair of shoes I fondled in my hands. They were pale blue, with a three inch heel and a peeptoe.

'It's like Cinderella,' I tried to joke in the excitement of fastening the buckles on the slingback straps. They were a bit too big for me but if I fastened them on the last hole, they didn't slip off my feet.

'Oh, they do fit,' said Pat, turning her head for a second from the wardrobe, where she was searching purposefully through Maureen's clothes.

'Well, they're quite a bit too big really,' I replied, not wanting to admit to having feet the size of boats, '...but I can manage to walk in them.' And I could. It was great. I'd dressed up in Mum's shoes loads of times but no matter how much you pretended, you could always hear the clip-clop of the high heel dragging behind as you pushed around the floor. In Maureen's shoes I felt grown up. I wasn't pretending to be grown up. It was lovely. I walked slowly across the carpet and swivelled like models do. I wanted Pat to see how naturally and easily I wore the shoes but she was far too busy struggling into a maroon, pencil slim skirt. It looked alarmingly new.

'I've been dying to try this on all week. She only bought it last Saturday. In fact she hasn't worn it yet. Nice, isn't it?'

Pat preened herself in front of the mirror. I stared with envy at the slim skirt she had pulled tight across her narrow hips.

'You try something on. Go on, take your pick,' she offered generously.

It was only when we were covering up our traces that I felt nervous again, and guilty. It was wrong, I supposed, but as Pat had said, we hadn't done any harm, had we? I wouldn't do it again, I decided. But the temptation was too great when, the following afternoon, Pat said: 'Shall we put make-up on this time, as well?'

Eventually, we made up little dramas. Wearing Maureen's clothes, Maureen's make-up and with Maureen's unlit cigarettes in our mouths, we rehearsed how we thought we'd be when we were older and our legs filled out the tops of Maureen's stockings. It took us longer and longer to achieve an authentically grown up appearance. The make-up and cigarettes had satisfied us for some time, but the real landmarks were undoubtedly the sock filled bras and stockings and suspender belts. We were treading dangerous ground here, since we had to use safety pins to make the bras and suspender belts fit. To reduce the risk of discovery we only used those that had been put out for the wash. Pat assured me that washing closed up the holes made by the pins.

To our eyes the transformation was marvellous. We were time travellers. Within minutes we were famous stars meeting adoring fans, beautiful women accepting invitations to dinner, a happy couple declaring their love for each other and sealing it with a kiss. This really did feel like stepping into adult territory. For a short while, the magic and mystery of being grown up were known to us.

One thing that spoiled the pleasure of the fantasy for me was the recognition that, in spite of being smaller and slighter, Pat always looked more grown up than me. It puzzled and niggled me. The clothes actually fitted me better and yet I still looked like a child dressed up as a woman.

Pat didn't. Even with a skirt and sweater almost wrapped around her thin body twice, she simply looked like a small woman. I decided that she knew how to use make-up better than I did. That must be it. But deep down, I felt it was connected with the reason why Pat had boyfriends and I didn't. It had something to do with her prettiness. Perhaps I had thought dressing up would hide the differences. Perhaps I had even thought that my size and build would give me an advantage over her. The dissatisfaction with myself grew and I realized that Pat was fussing over me.

'Here, you could do with a bit more up there,' tweaking my padded chest.

And on another occasion, watching me applying lipstick: 'I shouldn't use red, if I were you, it makes you look common.'

I'm sure she didn't mean anything by it. 'Common' was Pat's favourite word. She was always saying it about their Maureen because she wore too much make-up and smoked in the street and let her boyfriend, Dave, touch her inside her blouse when he kissed her good night. But somehow, it was all spoiled.

I didn't go round to her house for a couple of days. I didn't want to play dressing up any more and didn't know how to get out of it. On the third day, she called for me.

'Will you come round? I've got something to show you. It's brilliant. My mum finished it last night.'

She was so excited, I had to go.

'There. What do you think?'

She was waltzing around the living room floor pressing a full-skirted white lace dress in at her waist with one hand and the coathanger which held it in the other.

'Oh Pat, it's lovely. What's it for?'

As she spun round, I could see purple taffeta and wanted a closer look at the dress.

Pat stood still in front of me. 'It's for a talent competition at the Stargazer's Club, next Saturday. I'm going to do "Who's Sorry Now?" like I did at Butlin's last year. Only, I've grown out of my old dress, so my mum's made me a new one. She only started it Wednesday night and it's reversible, look.'

Quickly, she whipped the bodice through the skirt and there was a taffeta dress in front of me.

'The skirt's a full circle. You should see it spin.'

I fingered the silky material and turned it over in my hand to the white lace underside. 'It's so lovely on both sides, however will you decide which side to wear it?'

She must have sensed my longing. 'If it would fit you, I would let you try it on.' Then, in a rush, she said, 'I know. You choose. Whichever side you prefer, I'll wear for the competition.'

With mixed feelings, I agreed. She hadn't said anything about the competition when it had been announced at the Granada Saturday afternoon cinema club we went to most weeks. Why hadn't she mentioned it at the time? Why hadn't she asked me if I was going to enter? I'd known about the Butlin's competition, of course, but she hadn't won, only come third, I think.

She'd done the routine before, at several birthday parties, including my own. People were always impressed by the way she put the song over, rather than with her singing voice. She almost shouted it and did a lot of eye rolling and finger wagging which made her look rather 'cute' as my Auntie Bet put it. 'A proper little madam,' my grandma had said. 'Cheeky,' someone else had pronounced. But they had all enjoyed the confidence of the performance.

I suppose I'd forgotten about it really. Mrs Widdowson had chosen me to sing the solos in the Christmas concert, not Pat. But this reminder of the difference between our talents was disconcerting. Why hadn't I entered this competition myself? If I was such a good singer, why wasn't I getting a costume ready for the Grand Stargazer's Talent Competition?

'Come on, Pat, which side?'

'The purple, I think, yes, the purple.' I tried to sound enthusiastic.

As she struggled into the dress, I made myself more unhappy by answering the questions I had just asked. For a start, I hadn't the nerve. Secondly, there was nothing I could do. I only knew school songs, and no kid would want to pay good money to listen to another kid sing boring old school songs they'd been forced to learn at school. They paid their money to escape from school. That's what the films were all about. Pat and I had the same dream but she was the one who had the qualifications for a Hollywood musical, not me, and she was the one with the nerve to do something about it. She might even get her name in the *Advertiser*, our local paper.

'Can you do the zip up for me, Pat?' she said, turning her back to me.

The zip pulled the smooth taffeta snugly across her small back. The narrow bodice and full skirt emphasized the neatness of her head, shoulders and limbs. She looked beautiful. At that moment, I envied her more than I had ever done. Never would I look like that. Even when I was grown up, when everything that was wrong now would be put right, I was not going to look like that. Maureen's clothes had proved that to me. And Pat knew it too, just as she knew that the talent competition wasn't my sort of thing. That's why she hadn't mentioned it. Not because she was afraid I would do better than her.

We were both startled by a knock at the door. Pat hurriedly scooped up her clothes from the floor and placed them neatly on the sofa. She ran into the kitchen. 'Who's there?' she called, with her hand on the key. We'd got into the habit of locking the door.

'Is that you, Pat? It's Uncle Jack. What are you doing with the door locked?'

I'd only seen Pat's Uncle Jack once before but he was so much like Mr Baker there was no mistaking the family connection. Ignoring me, he walked straight through into the living room and sat heavily on the settee. I wondered if I should go. Then he smiled at both of us.

'Keeping house, are you? Looking after things, while everybody's out at work? Well, everything looks nice and tidy, I must say. You're a good girl, you know.'

Only now did he notice the dress Pat was wearing. 'That's a pretty dress, my duck. A bit too nice to be playing in or tidying up in, isn't it?'

'Don't be daft, Uncle Jack. I'm only trying it on to show Pat. It's for a talent competition at the Granada on Saturday. My mum made it,' and she twirled again in the middle of the floor, to show off the full charms of the dress.

Uncle Jack leaned forward on the settee. 'Very nice, my duck. I always said our Mary was a clever woman.' And stretching his hand out; 'It looks nice material. Come here a bit. Let's have a good look at it.'

Pat seemed less excited about the dress as she edged closer to Uncle Jack's outstretched hand. With both hands, he stroked the loose folds of the skirt. 'Nice bit of stuff, my duck. Colour suits you an' all.' Then, so swiftly that both of us were taken aback, he flicked up the hem of the dress. 'Have you got purple knickers to match, then?'

I felt myself flush, not because of the actual words, but because I didn't expect somebody's Uncle to talk like that.

'Come here, let's have a look at them.'

Pat ducked back, as he snatched at her hips. Just slipping out of his grasp, she ran behind the settee. Balancing on her finger tips, she was ready to spring in either direction. Uncle Jack crouched in front of the sofa, watching her swaying from side to side. Both of them were smiling, both of them were breathing hard. I stood watching, unable to do anything else, and understanding nothing of the scene before me, except that their smiles were not the same, their breathlessness was different.

He moved first. With a great roar, then a mocking, 'I'm coming to get you,' he pawed at the settee cushions and edged his way round towards her.

Pat screamed, half in fear, half in play: 'No, Uncle Jack, no.' She danced on her toes, weaving like a boxer.

'Come on, my duck. I'm not going to hurt you, am I? What are you running away for?'

Then, whilst Pat half choked a nervous giggle, he leapt round the back of the settee. She escaped his grasp again and they sped round the settee. I knew that I'd got a great, big, stupid grin on my face as if I was watching a Laurel and Hardy film, as though by smiling, I could keep things normal and safe.

Uncle Jack was oblivious to my smile, oblivious to me. His face was flushed and he laughed out loud as he chased Pat round the furniture. With childlike carelessness, he pushed a dining chair out of his way and it toppled over, brushing my leg as it fell.

The movement charged my body with fear. I knew something was wrong. I wanted to stop it, to stop Uncle Jack, to make him behave like the adults I knew. Pat might be giggling but she was afraid. I felt that to go would be to desert her, but I had to get out. I struggled to say something, knowing that nothing would sound right.

'Pat, I think I'll...'

I swallowed, shifted slightly towards the door and tried again.

'Pat, I think my mum's shouting for me.'

I repeated it, partly because I felt so much better for saying it, and partly because I thought they hadn't heard me. Just thinking about my mum made me feel safer.

Pat glanced at me, hesitated, and was caught. I was horrified. Uncle Jack had gripped her left arm with one hand and was struggling to secure her with the other. Pat punched at his free hand, half screaming and, strangely to me, half giggling still.

'Stop it, Uncle Jack. Stop it!'

More excited than ever, he fought to pull her even closer. 'Give us a kiss, just a little one.' His voice was low and wheedling but his knuckles were white where he grasped her.

There was a sharp intake of breath, Pat's face froze and her voice cut through the air: 'I shall tell me dad, Uncle Jack, I mean it, I shall tell him,' she threatened.

The game was over. Uncle Jack relaxed his hold immediately and she pushed his hand away. 'It was only a bit of fun, you know.'

She cut him short, 'I mean it, I shall tell him if you try to do anything again.'

Suddenly aware of my presence, Uncle Jack rather sheepishly smoothed his hair and jacket.

'Have you got last night's *Advertiser?* Oh, I see it. I'll get it.'

Sitting down with the paper, he gave Pat a little smile.

'Make me a cup of tea, duck, will you? Then I shall have to go.'

'I haven't got much time,' Pat warned. 'I've got to go to the shop for my mum soon.'

I went into the kitchen with Pat and left as she was busy filling the kettle.

It struck me that she didn't need me. She was in charge of the situation, just as she was in charge of the house while her parents were out at work. Minutes earlier, when I had felt that she was in danger, I had been powerless to help her. She had saved herself, and now she was behaving as if nothing had happened. I was the one who was agitated.

Later that night, I was still going over the incident in my head, trying to work out why it had upset me so much. After all, nothing had happened to me. In fact, had anything really happened at all? In the end it wasn't Uncle Jack's behaviour, or even Pat's that preoccupied me. It was my own. Could I have stopped Uncle Jack if Pat hadn't? And if I were ever in that situation, would I be able to act to save myself? I just didn't know.

I was a long time getting to sleep that night. Whenever I thought about Pat, I felt pretty miserable about myself. Somehow, it didn't seem to count that I did better at school, took the lead in the school pantomime and was dinner money monitor. That was school and school was a long, long way away. School didn't count. What counted was this world, where Pat seemed to score all the points.

I didn't call for Pat the next day. Uncle Jack's face and voice haunted me and the house would still be full of him. There was nothing to go round for now anyway. Even before I knew about Pat entering the competition I was fed up with dressing up games, and Pat would be full of talk about Saturday. She might even want me to help her rehearse.

'Have you and Pat fallen out?' Mum asked me on the Thursday.

'No.' I could tell she expected me to say more but I couldn't.

'Well, if you've got nothing to do I can find you something.'

I hate washing pots but I found it a lot easier than I would have found talking about Pat's Uncle Jack.

On the Friday night, I bumped into Pat on the street. The

curls on her head were tighter and sleeker than ever. Mrs Baker was trotting by her side with an equally fancy hairdo.

'I've had my hair permed for tomorrow,' Pat said, swivelling her head for my approval.

'Yes and you're not going to ruin it by playing out,' snapped her mother, prodding her in the middle of her back.

'You'll come and see me won't you?'

'Of course I will,' I said, as her mother bustled her up their path.

I wouldn't have missed it for anything. Pat came second. She performed with great charm to loud applause, but the winner was a curvy girl with waist length blond hair. Dressed in a grass skirt and a garland of flowers, she danced Hawaiian style to a record and a deafening scream of wolf whistles. To be fair, Pat was more talented and just as pretty, but glamour won the day.

It was also an important day for me. Neither Pat, nor the Hawaiian dancer, would have been chosen by Mrs Widdowson for the school play or concert, but here they were performing in public and being appreciated by the young audience for more than musical talent alone. I simply wasn't in that league. I wasn't going to Hollywood. If I couldn't get up on the stage of my local cinema, how could I possibly hope to become a film star? I really envied Pat and the Hawaiian dancer the thrill of the limelight, the applause and the admiration, but as I walked out into the bright, Saturday afternoon sunshine, I knew it wasn't for me. Pat would have to revise her ambitions too if she wasn't ever going to actually win a competition.

She wasn't at all put out about coming second. I had waited for her, to tell her how good she had been and that she should have won.

'Anyone could do what she did,' and she dismissed the Hawaiian dancer with a sexy wiggle of her hips, a limp wave of her arms and a pouting of the lips. 'Anyway,' she continued, 'my mum says I can go to Ivy Ellis' for tap lessons and they put on much better shows.'

Without either of us saying anything, we stopped playing together after the competition, although we were still friendly and chatted on the street, or in the playground.

There was only one small thing that niggled me for a while afterwards. Pat seemed to have forgotten all about it and I didn't know how to raise the matter. In the end I decided that she could keep the pound we had saved for our fare to America.

THE BUTTERFLY CHART

BERTA FREISTADT

They moved across the playground towards her in a bunch and spread out in a ring around her, giggling and pushing each other. In the centre was the boy called Malcolm; he wasn't very big or very tall, but he seemed to tower over the circle without doing very much. The rest of them linked arms and chanted,

> 'Come on Willy
> She's such a silly,
> Come on Chilly
> She'll catch a cold.'

Roxy held her ground and didn't move. She was scared and angry. She was scared of what they might do to her, though what it was she didn't know, and she was angry because it was so unfair.

'My name's not Willy,' she muttered. She couldn't say it very loud because she would have to shout to make herself heard. She didn't want to shout, they might think she wanted to fight.

'My name's Roxy.'

Roxy's real name was Wilhelmina. Now you may laugh, or groan and say that no one is called Wilhelmina these days. But that's where you'd be wrong. If you had parents who were foreign and didn't care what anyone thought, and if Wilhelmina was a best aunt who'd looked after your dad when he'd been orphaned, then you might just get called that. Wilhelmina hadn't realized that there was anything wrong with her name until she'd gone to school. On the first day, the whole class had rocked with laughter when her name was called and even the teacher had a smile on her face. After that she hadn't bothered to make friends, because being laughed at by the whole class had seemed to her the worst thing in the whole world. No one laughed at her at home; in fact everyone there seemed rather serious a lot of the time. When Wilhelmina had tried to explain matters, her mother had said,

'Nonsense dear, Wilhelmina's a lovely name.'

And there didn't seem much point in arguing.

Wilhelmina had named herself Roxy one day, several years ago, for two reasons. Firstly, she'd seen the word on a cinema, though she hadn't at the time known what a cinema was. She was learning to read then and had read the word right off, though she'd never seen any word quite like it in any of her school reading books. Her mother was so pleased and proud, that she'd told everyone about her daughter's reading progress and Roxy had been praised so much, that every time she thought of the word it gave her a good feeling. The second reason was because her lovely Aunt Jane had a wonderful dog called Roxanne, or Roxy for short. Roxanne was small and white with cream bits. She was very licky and behaved in a dreadful way that made Roxy laugh. Roxy dog would sit under the table while they were eating with Aunt Jane's shoe in her mouth, with Aunt Jane's foot still in it. Aunt Jane thought this was a laugh too and made faces at Roxy which made her almost choke with laughter. Her parents didn't quite approve. They thought that hysteria at meal times wasn't quite the thing, but they loved Aunt Jane as much as Roxy did and, as they didn't eat with her that often, they frowned gently at Roxy and smiled patiently at Aunt Jane.

So it had occurred to her, one day, that Roxy was obviously the name for her. It made her feel good and she hoped that the thought of Roxy dog under the table biting things, would make her feel braver. Mind you, no one ever called her Roxy, mainly because she never told anyone. At home she was still called Wilhelmina and at school they called her a variety of things. Willy mainly. They seemed to think that the word Willy was especially funny, though Roxy couldn't for the life of her see why. Sometimes, they called her Chilly Willy because of the thick tights and jumpers she wore in the winter. None of the other girls seemed to wear thick clothes even in the cold. Most of their parents had cars and they got picked up after school. Roxy walked. It wasn't far, in fact, you could see the school gate from the upstairs bedroom in their house. Her parents thought she would catch colds if she wasn't warmly dressed. Roxy agreed, she hated to feel cold, but even more she hated to be called names. When she did tell her mother all about it one day, her mother was upset about the names but told her that was nothing, compared to what some people had to put up with elsewhere in the world. Roxy didn't need to be told this: she watched the news on the TV and heard her parents argue about politics on a Sunday morning. One day her mother came back from the library down the road with a book of English rhymes. Roxy could tell she was pleased because her mother, usually so pale and serious, was flushed and smiling. She opened the book and showed Roxy what she'd found; it was a short rhyme of two lines.

'Sticks and stones may break my bones
But names will never hurt me.'

Roxy was disappointed. That's all her mother knew, but she learnt it, for something to do and to reassure her mother, who seemed to think that this rhyme was like a magic spell; if you knew it, you could throw it at your enemies and everything would be all right. But it didn't stop the names and it didn't stop her feeling like crying every time it happened. When they all gathered round her, she couldn't even get the rhyme out.

She'd said, 'My name is Roxy,' very quietly, for her own sake really and she'd thought very hard about Roxanne's teeth. But, somehow the girl nearest to her had heard.

'Oh!' she shrieked. 'Her name's Roxy!' and then, 'Roxy, Roxy, who's got a poxy!'

Roxy fixed her eyes on the clock above the entrance to the school. It always said ten forty-five. She began to feel hotter and a kind of empty buzzing filled her ears as she gripped the railing behind her.

'Roxy! Roxy! who's got a poxy!' The laughter grew louder and the shapes of the children before her seemed to dance right up into the sky. Suddenly, 'Leave her alone.' It was Malcolm. There was immediate silence, like a radio being switched off. Roxy could hear the noise her breathing was making, rough and rasping. She wondered if they could hear the throbbing that was inside her too. For a long while the silence held and they stared at each other. The crowd stared at Roxy, as if she was something they had invented and Roxy and Malcolm stared at each other, as if there was no one else in the playground. As her breathing got quiet, she could hear a train from the railway and longed to be on it going anywhere: to London, to China, to the moon. And then she heard the dog. Far away in the distance the sound of a little dog's yapping.

'Let it be Roxanne,' she silently begged to herself, to an angel, to God, to her fairy godmother. 'Let it be my darling Roxy dog come to rescue me.'

Then, as she thought of pictures of Roxanne biting the invisible chains that bound her, Malcolm smiled and came towards her.

'Come on,' he said, 'you know what you've got to do.'

Roxy shuddered. She did indeed know. They told her that very first day. 'What you have to do,' they said, 'is kiss Malcolm, and then you're in his gang.' She thought about it now. Would it be worth it? It's only a kiss and then she'd be in a gang, safe. But she felt stubborn. She knew this was her last chance, but she was filled with the unfairness of it. There were boys in the gang and they didn't have to do any kissing. She looked at Malcolm and thought,

'I won't!'

His pale face swam before her. Her Aunt Jane would call him pasty. 'More like pastry' said a little voice inside her. 'Kiss him!' said the little voice, 'not likely'. Her lips went small and tight and her mouth couldn't help turning down at the corners. 'You don't want to kiss a pastry,' said the little voice getting quite bold now, nearly making Roxy laugh. As if sensing the change in her, as if sensing what was in her head, he flushed and stepped forward, angrily. As he came closer, some of the girls closed up together, giggling and laughing, breaking the silence. The dog barked again, nearer this time and in a moment, Roxy leapt forward, pushing Malcolm aside. Keeping her eye on the gap in the circle the girls had made, she threw her body into the space and out the other side. At that moment, the teacher rang the bell for afternoon school and Roxy darted into the safety of her classroom.

'If only I had a gang,' Roxy thought, 'or at least if I was in someone else's.' The whole school seemed to be made up of different gangs. First there was the teachers against the children, then there was the boys against the girls. Then there were all the age groups and inside those, were the groups who could do the work and those who could not. But those were only the official gangs. Outside in the playground there were divisions that cut across the school's arrangements. Sometimes children hung out together from the same street, or in families, or because they all liked football or animals or Elvis Presley. Roxy didn't care what it was, except for kissing Malcolm she'd have taken up wellington boot throwing if they'd have asked her, but they didn't. In the classroom it wasn't so bad, but in the playground she stood either alone, or surrounded by jeering faces.

A few weeks after she'd refused to kiss Malcolm, a new girl joined the class and for a while Roxy felt some relief that this girl was the new face. She felt as if a burning spotlight had been taken off her and one or two girls actually spoke to her without calling her names. She began to enjoy going to school. The new girl's name was Miriam and she had foreign parents too. She had a brother, but he was much younger and in a different class. Roxy watched them both, as they stood in the playground alone on their first day. At first they stood by the door, but a teacher shooed them away and into the middle of the playground.

'Go and play,' she said. 'Run around and get some exercise.' From her watch point, Roxy saw the two of them wander aimlessly as though they were floundering knee deep in water to the middle of the yard. They stood there holding hands, like uncertain animals. Roxy could see what was going to happen. From all points of the compass, the members of Malcolm's gang slowly surrounded them. For a moment Roxy thought she would run over and rescue them, but something stopped her. It wasn't just fear. It wasn't just to safeguard her new position in the class. She really wanted to see what would happen; to watch it happen to someone else. Anyway, holding hands! They were really asking for it.

The group was right round the two newcomers and Roxy could hear some laughter and a low chant begin. She couldn't make out the words of the jeering, but she knew the tune. Then suddenly there was the sound of a slap and someone screamed. Roxy heard the sound of weeping and thought, 'They've gone too far this time.' Some of the group scattered and Roxy looked into the centre. She was surprised. It wasn't Miriam who was crying. No, she was standing there tall with her hand out like a flag, in a fist. Another girl was in tears, being comforted by friends.

In the days that followed, no one teased or taunted Miriam or her little brother. No one approached them at all. It was as if they were invisible and not even Roxy went near them. Roxy felt bad when she thought of that moment when she'd just let it happen. 'I'm as bad as they are,' she thought. There was a strange feeling to school after Miriam had stood up for herself. In the classroom everyone was quieter than usual, and in the playground at playtime, it felt as if someone was holding their breath. Then two things happened. First, they began to call Roxy names again: Chilly Willy and Roxy Poxy. That was bad enough, but there was also something awful happening to Miriam. Roxy couldn't quite put her finger on it, for it wasn't exactly jeering and it wasn't actual name calling and what was more, it didn't just happen in the playground. Sometimes, in the classroom, Miriam would flush under her golden skin and look tense and Roxy would know that something had happened. Some comment, some remark, some word had hurt her. Roxy would often be right there when it happened and still she couldn't tell what it was. She knew without looking at Miriam that something was going on by the faces of the gang. She could see the looks they gave each other and how their mouths were clamped tight on secret smiles. Roxy began to feel sorry for Miriam when she wasn't busy looking after herself and soon everything was back to normal and Roxy hated school again.

One day, Aunt Jane invited Roxy over for tea. A Halloween tea. They'd done Halloween at school, sticking cut out broomsticks and witches hats and cats on the windows. They'd also had to write a story about a witch. Roxy thought it was a bit pointless. When she got to Aunt Jane's though, it really did look spooky and even little Roxy dog seemed more subdued than usual. All the curtains were drawn and Aunt Jane was dressed in black and had glittery eye make-up on. On the table were hollow pumpkins with eyes that winked from candles inside them. There were green sandwiches, green jelly and a cake in the shape of a cat, covered with black icing. Despite this, it all tasted delicious and even better, they didn't have to do the washing up afterwards like they usually did. Instead Aunt Jane pushed the tea table into a corner and put some cushions on the floor.

'Let's make a spell,' she said and pulled Roxy onto the floor.

Roxy dog wanted to join the party but she was banished to her own cushion by the radiator in the window.

Roxy sat on the cushion. She was definitely feeling a bit nervous; what on earth was going on? She watched Aunt Jane put a metal tray between them that had a box on it. It was a big old box with a carved lid that showed four birds with outstretched wings, one in each corner. Roxy had seen it many times, it usually sat by Aunt Jane's bed and held her diary and pills and tissues and things. This time when she opened it, Aunt Jane brought out a long filmy black scarf which she flipped into the air and brought floating like a cloud around Roxy's shoulders.

'Now you're a witch too,' she said.

Then out of the box came a black bowl, a black jug, a wooden spoon, some coloured candles and some little brown glass bottles Roxy had never seen before.

'What spell shall we cast?' said Aunt Jane, looking at Roxy.

Suddenly from feeling a bit awkward, because she knew Aunt Jane wasn't really a witch and that the spoon belonged in the kitchen, Roxy began to feel a little breathless as though something was going to happen. Perhaps it was because Aunt Jane had stopped smiling at her and had asked the question very seriously, as though she meant it. In fact, Aunt Jane hadn't taken her eyes off Roxy since she'd spoken and Roxy was feeling that she might drown in Aunt Jane's eyes if she wasn't careful. She'd never noticed before that they were green as a cat's, she'd always thought Aunt Jane had brown eyes, like everyone else in the family. 'Spell' thought Roxy.

'Well, I don't know,' she said aloud, though inside for some reason her heart had begun to pound and pound.

'What do you want most in the whole world, Roxy?' said Aunt Jane, which was strange, for she didn't think she'd told Aunt Jane her new name. 'Do you want riches, or beauty, or brains, or courage?'

Courage! Immediately she knew why her heart was beating. She knew that was what she was going to say before the words had even formed in her head. This was the moment she'd been waiting for, even though she'd never planned it, or thought of it, or even expected it to happen. She looked right back at the witch and said, 'Courage!' as loudly as she dared. In the bay window the little dog sighed in his sleep and his paws twitched as if he were chasing cats. The witch smiled and stood up. Opening one of the brown bottles she tipped it and poured a shining white powder onto the floor. Walking round in a circle with the bottle, she drew a white ring around them and said,

'Now we're safe.'

She put the bowl before Roxy and from the jug she poured some water into it.

'Look at your face in the water,' said the witch and Roxy bent over and peered into the dark puddle.

Suddenly her face was there and on either side, sparking and glittering, were two red candles that seemed to have lit themselves. Looking at her face as it swam between the two lights, Roxy began to feel strange; dizzy, as though the top of her head didn't belong to her. From a long way away a voice said softly,

'Pour all your tears and fears into the water, Roxy, dig them out of your heart and flush them away.'

As she tried to do this there came from nowhere the soft wind rustling leaves and birds twittering in the distance.

'Now close your eyes and think of the bravest person you know.'

This took Roxy a lot longer than pouring her tears and fears away, because first of all she couldn't remember anyone brave at all, until she remembered Joan of Arc. Just as she was wondering if Joan of Arc had dark or blonde hair, the image of Miriam, standing with her hand out after the slap, came into her head, so she decided to have her. After all, Miriam was younger than Joan which must make her braver and although Miriam had her brother to help her, he was scarcely older than a baby and Joan of Arc had the whole French army. So there wasn't much of a contest as to who was the bravest.

It was easy after that. She had to breathe Miriam's picture into the bright flame of a red candle while the witch unscrewed two more brown bottles. From one she dripped ten drops of a golden liquid into the black bowl of water and slowly, lowered the red Miriam candle until the flame touched the water. In a moment the bowl was alight with fire; a blue flame seemed to hover like the shadow of a ghost above the bowl. There was a soft howl from the window and Roxy could see Roxy dog shift and stir, her nose twitching as she went back to sleep. Roxy's eyes widened at the flame; she'd never been allowed to 'play with fire,' as her mother called it. As the flame died down, the witch took a pinch of something scarlet from the other bottle and threw it into the last of the fire. It sparkled and cracked like a small voice laughing and finally the water cleared and was still.

'Drink.' said the witch and lifted the bowl in her two hands and offered it to Roxy.

It wasn't hot as she'd expected, but she looked into the green eyes of the witch with a little doubt.

'Is it poison?' she said shyly, she didn't want to seem ungrateful. The green eyes narrowed for a moment and then the witch laughed softly.

'No, it's a cup of courage. Drink.'

So she drank.

The water tasted bitter and stung her lips for a second, but in the next it was almost fragrant and reminded her of winter, of something you had when it was cold.

'One more thing,' said the green eyes, 'do you know the face of your enemy?'

Roxy nodded immediately. Of course she did.

'Good, put that picture into this flame,' and she lit another candle, a grey one this time. As the flame of the grey candle flickered and grew, Roxy saw Malcolm's pastry face and his satisfied smile.

'Count to ten and blow it out,' said the witch.

Roxy frowned. That seemed a bit drastic.

'Won't that kill him?'

'Only in your head,' said the witch. 'Go ahead and count.'

So again she did what the witch said.

'One, two, three, four, five...'

She paused at nine, feeling this was a very serious thing to do. She did so want to be brave. She wanted to be as brave as Miriam when she had defended herself; she was tired of being scared, of being ashamed of herself.

Roxy paused. She thought she heard Roxy dog give a soft bark, as if telling her to move on and she remembered Roxy dog's little teeth.

'...Nine, ten.'

She closed her eyes tightly and blew. She'd always been good at blowing out candles; all nine had gone first blow at her last party. In fact, she'd blown so hard that there were little flecks of wax all over the icing on the cake. She opened her eyes and he was gone. Malcolm. She couldn't see him any more. The witch had gone too and in her place was a lovely Aunt Jane, all full of smiles with her arms out.

'Don't look so serious,' she said, leaning over the box and the bottles and the smoking candles to give Roxy a great, big hug.

At this, Roxy dog got up, stretched and yawned and trotted over to his little friend. She took the end of the black silk scarf in her mouth and, wagging her tail at speed, put her head on one side with the look in her eye that said, 'Let's play.' So they did.

It was in a nature lesson when it all blew up. It felt like a volcano; she remembered thinking that while she was in the middle of it all. Not that she'd ever been in one, but they'd seen a film and done some drama about it. A volcano starts with rumbling beneath your feet and the air gets hot and full of grits, then suddenly, there is the explosion and down the side of the mountain comes lava, fast and dangerous, killing everything in its way. Nobody did get killed, quite, but at the same time it felt like it.

At first there was nothing. Everyone was finishing off a project on water. There was a feeling in the room, as there often was at the end of the day, of doing something good. Roxy was working on her own, as usual, and only had to put the page numbers at the bottom of each page. The others were finishing drawings and one or two were tidying up the class library, putting back the books they'd used during the project. At twenty minutes to the bell, the teacher began to pin up a big chart onto the board, in readiness for the lesson after the break. It was the prettiest chart Roxy had ever seen. Everyone made a loud 'Ooo' sound together. The chart was covered with butterflies. They seemed to fly around the border; a million of them in colours bright and pale. The chart was a shiny one so that as the afternoon sun caught the paper they really seemed to be alive. In the centre, a giant butterfly flew with wings outstretched, like a great blue bird.

Almost everyone in the class had stopped and had turned to watch the chart as the final drawing pin was stuck in.

'What's that, Miss?' said someone.

Underneath the huge butterfly were a couple of other things, one dry and wrinkled like an old leaf and the other soft and fluffy like a skinny ball of wool.

'After break,' said the teacher.

'Oh go on, Miss, just tell us what those things are.'

The teacher was putting her things into her bag, ready to leave the room to get a cup of tea, but she stopped for a moment and smiled.

'You are keen,' she said. 'The wrinkly thing is a chrysalis and the fluffy one is the cocoon.'

There was a sudden change of temperature. Then a few isolated things happened, one after the other so that they became connected. Two girls looked at each other and smiled. Miriam, who was fastening a shoe lace stopped and looked up and Malcolm's head turned to look at Miriam. It was like a dance. One, two, three. Then the rumbling seemed to begin. Someone snickered in the corner and across the other side of the room, someone else said,

'A coon, Miss?'

The teacher laughed,

'No dear, a cocoon. We'll find out all about it after play.'

'A funny colour for a coon,' said Malcolm, looking at Roxy and smiling pleasantly.

Roxy knew that this was an important moment. She wasn't sure why. It had something to do with Miriam and that thing on the board. If only she could understand what was going on she'd know what to do. Why was Malcolm smiling at her all of a sudden?

'Isn't it?' he said softly. 'Coons aren't that colour, are they?' He was looking at her with such intensity, that Roxy began to feel afraid. She wished the teacher would do something, but she was straightening her desk.

'Whose side are you on?' he said. 'Ours or theirs?'

Before she could answer, before she could say how can the cocoon have a side, there was a kind of roaring sound and Roxy saw Miriam stand up, pulling herself to her full height. She saw Miriam launch herself into the air.

'Don't call me that!' she screamed and landed on Malcolm's back.

All of a sudden, in an explosion of fists and tears and shouting, Roxy understood.

The word 'coon'. She'd heard it over the past few weeks, muttered and whispered by the gang members. When she thought about it now, Miriam was always in earshot when the word was said. She understood that somehow, 'coon' was the same for Miriam, as Chilly Willy was for her. Suddenly she was filled with an enormous anger and joy. It happened in a flash, her brain put everything together and she knew which side she was on. The only thing was that it was too late. She'd been too slow, she'd missed the point. Missed the boat, as her dad sometimes said as he rushed out of the house late for work. Though why the boat, when he went by bus, Roxy could never understand. Now, the air before her was full of fists punching and legs kicking. Chairs had been knocked over and a ring of children surrounded the fight. Only the teacher, like herself, stood still and silent, obviously as shocked as Roxy. Suddenly, as if remembering something, she seemed to pull herself together and pushing forward she reached into the fight and grabbed a bit of each child.

'That's enough!' she shouted, her voice full of anger as the two fighters fell apart, hair messed and clothes ripped.

They crouched opposite each other, panting, their eyes flashing at each other.

'How dare you!' said the teacher, in the loudest voice Roxy had ever heard her use. 'In my class! How dare you. I will not have fighting. That's for the baby class. You want to fight? Go to the baby class. And the rest of you. Standing round enjoying it. I've never seen anything more disgusting in my life. Malcolm...' she turned to him, '...you've let me down. I always thought I could trust you.' She looked at Miriam. 'As for you, what would your parents think? Did you think of that?'

Roxy thought that was unfair. It was like a threat, somehow; but the teacher continued.

'I couldn't believe my eyes. You deliberately jumped on his back, I saw you. What ever did you do that for?'

But Miriam stayed silent. Her face was wet, but she wasn't crying any more. She ignored the teacher who held her by one arm and was still watching Malcolm as if she was afraid to let him out of her sight.

'Well, answer me, Miriam,' said the teacher. 'What have you to say?'

Roxy waited. 'Come on, Miriam,' she thought, '...tell her.' But Miriam said nothing.

Roxy began to feel miserable. She felt tears building up because something awful was happening. If Malcolm got away with this.... She looked at him and saw that he was looking at Miriam as hard as she looked at him; but with a difference. Where Miriam's mouth was tight and hard and unhappy, at the corner of Malcolm's mouth, Roxy saw the tiniest lift of a smirk. That did it! In a flash she saw again the flame of the grey candle and before she knew what she was doing, or could count the cost, she'd said,

'It was his fault, Miss.'

She said it so loudly that she surprised herself. All the heads turned to look at her and Malcolm's smile vanished. In its place came a look of complete surprise and Miriam's mouth stopped being a thin hard line. The teacher let go of Miriam's arm and said,

'Wilhelmina? What do you know about this?'

And so Roxy told her. In front of them all. About the names and the jeering and Miriam and the word coon, which she still didn't understand, only how it would feel to Miriam. There was a shocked hush while she was speaking and one or two of the children went and sat down. A couple of girls began to cry, as though they knew trouble was on the way and that it would come to all of them. While Roxy was speaking, she knew she was breaking some sort of rule and that she'd probably have to face up to it in the playground later, but she couldn't stop once she'd started. If she stopped talking, she knew she'd burst into tears and she could feel Miriam's eyes on her and wanted, above all things, not to cry now.

When it was over, when she'd finished speaking, the bell went as if to mark the end of something, but no one moved. The teacher was silent for a moment and then she turned and unpinned the chart.

'We'll do this next week,' she said. 'When you come back, after play, I want to talk to all of you.'

They all trooped out and only Roxy and Miriam were left. The teacher tried to straighten up Miriam's clothes but she wouldn't let her. Miriam had lost two buttons which the teacher found lying under a desk where the fight had happened. Miriam would only accept the needle and cotton from the teacher.

'Thank you, Miss, I'll do it later.'

It felt as though Miriam was dismissing her. Then she turned to Roxy and said,

'I've got to go and meet my brother, d'you want to come?'

Her brother was waiting anxiously by the door. Miriam took his hand and the three of them went and stood by the railings. Playtime was nearly over. Roxy noticed the little boy eyeing his sister's missing buttons and wondered why he didn't mention them. Neither Miriam, nor Roxy spoke, they just stood with their backs to the railings and watched the playground. Then in the distance, Roxy heard the little dog bark. It gave a long series of yaps, as if it were having an argument. The little boy smiled suddenly and said,

'I wish we had a dog, Mirry.'

She looked at him and smiled back,

'One day,' she said.

Suddenly everything felt better. The air was easier to breathe, the sky was bluer and standing in a threesome felt just right. No one in their right mind would have a go at three people. She laughed out loud and the others looked at her.

'My Aunt Jane's got a lovely dog. I could ask her if we could all take her out for a walk..'

They looked at each other and Miriam nodded. Then the bell went and they slowly walked across the playground, preparing themselves for the talking to that the teacher had promised.

FIRST COMMUNION

GER DUFFY

They were late. The tiled corridors were empty. As they crept up the stairs, the chanting of multiplication tables and singing followed them. Tricia disappeared through her classroom door. Ann walked more slowly.

'...three four five six, I slept late, seven eight nine, the car wouldn't start.'

Her excuses seemed feeble. The smells of wax polish and chalk filled her nose as she entered the classroom. Sr Ignatius looked up from calling the register and frowned.

Since the Christmas holidays Sr Ignatius had been drilling the class in the catechism they, as first communicants, were expected to know. She walked back and forth across the front of the room, her stick, placed at an upward angle, pointed at the class. At first the questions were easy. Who made the world? Who is God? What are the ten commandments? Recite the creed. Ann still hadn't been asked. Six girls were already standing in the corner, for every answer missed they would receive two slaps on each hand. Anne tried to remember the creed.

'I believe in God the Father Almighty Maker of Heaven and Earth, Maker of all things something and something.'

Claire Hensey recited it perfectly. When Ann's turn arrived, the finger jumped over her.

'I'm not going to bother with girls who come in late.'

That evening, Ann went to Mrs Digan's to get fitted for her communion dress. While she waited in the hall, she could hear people talking behind the partition. Mam sat down as they waited, occasionally she pulled at the collar of her dress. Tricia delved through a mound of scrap material in a heap at the corner; although she had made her first communion the year before, she too was getting a new dress for the occasion. At last, the Larkins appeared from behind the partition and left. The partition was made out of chipboard, at one end stood a huge, old mirror, framed in dark wood. On ledges along the wall, were packets of pins, measuring tape, rolls of velcro, ribbons and linings. In the mirror, everyone looked broader and squarer than they really were. Mrs Digan hurried back, rushing through the curtained entrance so that it billowed after her. In the hall, people coughed and shuffled their feet. The material had been cut and tacked together hurriedly and looked the size and shape of brown, paper grocery bags. Trisha's was pink and Ann's was blue, turquoise blue, a name she'd never heard before, and Trisha's was cerise pink, Mrs Digan told them, pins clamped between her lips.

Since last month when the Parish Bulletin had stated that girls would not be restricted to wearing white for the First Communion ceremony, Mam had pored over the heavy dressmaking books in Mrs Digan's back room and examined all the shades and textures of the material in Melville's Drapery shop. Eventually she decided on a heavy crimplene material with white daisy trimming. Ann looked in the mirror. One sleeve was sewn on, the dress was held together with tacking and pins. She looked odd in it, half dressed. Ann didn't believe for one moment that this was going to be her first communion dress, and even if Mam was serious, there was Tricia's white dress from last year, though Tricia was smaller and fatter than her and Mam had said that Ann looked spindly in it.

At night, in the red spotted darkness behind her lids, she saw herself in Tricia's dress, gliding slowly to the altar. She felt the weight and awe of the veil on her head and the crown of plastic flowers intertwined. Somewhere Sr Ignatius was looking on approvingly saying,

'What a pious little girl Ann Doyle is, how strange I never noticed it before!'

In the run up to the big day, Sr Ignatius grew more and more excited. Hardly a day passed without everyone in the class receiving a slap. Ordinary subjects were forgotten. Catechism took from nine until two. The girls sat upright in the two by two desks. Gradually the pressure increased. Those who hesitated were removed from the line. Carmel Kilklein licked both hands furtively before being slapped, then ran back to her seat grinning, although her hands were tucked under her armpits. The class grew hot and sweaty, waiting to be asked. The Bracken twins created a diversion by fainting simultaneously, and when they recovered, vomited all over their jumpers. Sr Ignatius scattered sawdust at their feet. Although it was cold, they had to stand in their blouses, in front of the class, dishonoured. Just then a precise knock was heard. Sr Ignatius warned the class.

'Cuineas anios.' [Quiet now.]

The door was almost closed, the sharp tones of the Monsignor's contrasted with the lighter tones of the nun. Anyone who failed the oral examination would have to stay back a year and couldn't make their first communion until then. The Monsignor entered, followed by Sr Ignatius. She clapped her hands,

'What do you say, girls?'

'Good morning, Monsignor,' they chorused.

'Good morning, girls,' he snapped. 'A little bird told me you are all very hard working girls, is that true?'

Mary Sherlock nodded and said, 'Yes, Monsignor.'

'Hmm, we'll see. I'm sure you all know your catechism very well indeed by now.' He stopped and looked at the twins.

'Dear oh dear, what have we here at all?'

'They were ill just as you arrived, Monsignor,' Sr Ignatius stated, her hands clasped.

'Would you like to go home girls?' he barked. They shook their heads shyly.

'They are from the country, Monsignor, they will get the school bus home. Sit down girls.' They walked stiffly from the spot and sat in their desks.

'I hope you're not frightened of me,' he said with a laugh that stopped short.

'Of course not,' Sr Ignatius laughed in return.

'Well. Does anyone know the Lord's prayer?'

Every hand shot up, some even waved. Annette Daly stood up and said it, her hands devoutly pressed together.

'Well Sister, I think because they've all been so good, we can let them have the rest of the day off.'

A confused buzz ran through the class. The questions they'd learnt every night and recited every morning hung on their tongues. Ann ran home by herself for the first time ever.

Mam stood in the kitchen ironing.

'Why are you home so early?'

'We had the catechism exam, I ran all the way home, what's for dinner?'

Ann rummaged in her bag for the school note from Sr Ignatius, asking parents to ensure that the girls receiving First Communion be dressed in the traditional white. Mam read it with a slight smile, then crumpled it and put it in her pocket.

'Your dress has arrived.' The blue dress lay on her bed, next to the old white one covered in plastic.

'Do you like it?' asked Mam. Ann shook her head, tears threatening.

'I honestly can't think what you see in Tricia's old dress,' Mam continued.

'It's white, it's the one I'm supposed to wear.'

Mam laughed softly. 'Blue is nicer on you, you look peaky in white.'

'I don't care, I want to wear this one,' she held the white dress up close to her, 'I don't like that blue dress. I won't wear it.'

Footsteps came down the hall, Dad appeared over her shoulder.

'Now, now, that white doesn't suit you at all.'

Mam sniffed, 'After all my work this is the thanks I get.'

Dad looked at Ann and sighed, 'Now look what you've done, she's upset.'

Ann sat snivelling on the bed.

'Mam spent a lot of time and money, making sure you'd have a nice dress. That white dress is a tatty old thing.'

Ann bawled into the bedclothes,

'It's white,' she sobbed. How could she explain the image in her head, moving in white to the altar? The white dress had layers of faded lace, rows of pearl drops and buttons, even the crinkly feel of it moving against her fingers made her feel special. Who could feel holy in a turquoise dress with a sash of white daisies gathered at the waist?

'Why can't I wear the white one, why?'

Dad sighed,

'Look wear the blue one like a good girl, you want to be Daddy's girl, don't you?'

'I won't wear it, you want to make a holy show of me, I won't go at all.' She ran to where Mam sat in the dining room and shouted, 'I hate you, I hate you, I hate you.'

Mam said nothing, one hand was pressed to her forehead. Dad had come in behind Ann, he pulled her by the ear to the armchair.

'Now you see what I've to put up with, Sean?'

'How dare you speak to your mother like that, I won't have it, do you hear?'

Ann looked at him.

'Apologize and say you're sorry, apologize to your mother now.'

'No, I won't.'

'Right then,' he placed her over his knee. 'Take that and that, that'll teach you to have manners.'

'Go easy on her Sean, don't hurt her.'

Ann kicked and squirmed as the slaps hailed her bottom and she was ejected out the back door.

'You're not getting back in here until you apologize.'

Ann stood on the step hiccupping and crying. It still wasn't dinner time. She kicked and punched the back door for a while. Her nose dribbled and she began to get a headache. Mam came to the window, smiled and waved out at her. Ann stuck out her tongue and walked to the side of the house, where she couldn't be seen.

They marched two by two, to the church holding hands. As a class, they had never been outside the school yard before. The sounds and smells delighted and frightened them. It was market day and the squeal of the pigs, the smell of the cow dung and the sharp 'hup, hup' voices of farmers filled the air. Pair by pair they were hustled into the dark empty church. Two confessional boxes were available, the class filled six rows. The first two rows had to kneel and repent, the others could sit back until their turns came. Ann couldn't decide which of her sins to put first, she told lies, she stole, and she was disobedient. The door opened and she was nudged forward. It was completely dark. A metal grid faced her, perforated with tiny holes. It was the same black darkness as the ghost trains in Bray, she wouldn't have been surprised if a skeleton brushed past her. The shutter was pulled back, with a clattering noise.

'This is your first confession child?'

'Yes Father, I confess to Almighty God and to you, Father.'

His profile leaned towards her, one hand over his eyes, it was the Monsignor.

'And tell me, what sins do you wish to confess?'

'I told lies, I stole, I was disobedient, that's all Father.'

'These are all little sins, but if we don't try to curb them while we're young, they can lead to greater temptations. Now who were you disobedient to?'

'To my mother, Father,' said Ann, thinking of the dress.

'For your penance say the act of contrition.' He gabbled through her absolution in Latin and made the sign of the cross,

'Go in peace.'

The shutter drew across and Ann was left in complete darkness. She leant all her weight against the door and it opened suddenly. She stood in the aisle blinking, before being shuttled into a pew. Through slits in her fingers, Ann watched Annette Daly walk down the main aisle, to the cordoned off block of pews reserved for the class on Saturday. She shivered at the thought of the blue dress.

'Oh my God, I am heartily sorry, for all my sins.'

'Up, up, it's time to get up!' Dad shook her hurriedly, his back disappearing through the open doorway.

Turning on her side, she saw the dress covered in plastic hanging from the outside of the wardrobe. Piled in little mounds on the dressing table were the soft heap of white socks, knickers, vest and slip. A long, rectangular white cardboard box at the end of the bed, contained her veil. Curlers dug into her scalp, especially where her head lay on the pillow.

'Do I have to call you again, Ann?' his voice came, from further down the hall.

'No, Dad, I'm up now,' her voice shouted back easily, as she lay on her back and stretched.

'Are you not dressed yet?' Mam watched her from the doorway.

'Will you take these out?' Ann sat in front of the dresser, pulling at the curlers. Mam quickly undid them and Ann's hair fell down like unfinished rope. As Mam used her forefinger and brush, large sausage ringlets appeared that bounced on either side of Ann's head. Mam parted the hair in the middle, then looped the ringlets back from her face with clips.

'There, you look lovely.'

Ann's hair felt strange and light, the ringlets tickled her cheeks and neck. Her fingers squashed one, it was quite soft yet kept its shape, she hated them. The dress hung glittering behind the plastic. Cold lining clung to her skin, as she stepped into it. She had said the rosary every night for the past month to save her from this moment, but it was no use. In the kitchen Tricia stopped spooning her cornflakes and stared at her.

'You look a sight.'

Ann made a face, and sat down pushing dry cereal around her bowl. His head appeared in the door,

'Get a move on, or we'll never get there.'

In the hall, Mam fussed over the veil. She placed it over the ringlets with clips,

'I'll fix it better in the car.'

White gloves and a black handbag were thrust into her hands. She sat in the car motionless. Either there was a God or there wasn't. If there was he would stop this right now; if there wasn't, well at least she'd know. Mam turned around in the front and threw Holy water over them as Dad revved the engine and reversed the car out the gate. Everything familiar flashed past. Her hands and armpits sweated as the car went faster and faster. Suddenly a dark shape hit the windscreen and slumped onto the bonnet. Mam and Tricia screamed, the car wavered and screeched to a halt. Blood and feathers hung congealed on the windscreen. Mam and Tricia turned their tear stained faces at Dad.

'Damn and blast, are we ever going to get anywhere on time? It's only a bird for Christ's sake, Kate, a bloody bird.'

Mam sniffed into her handkerchief.

'We got a fright, that's all.'

Dad opened the door, Mam pushed a wad of tissues at him,

'In case of germs.'

He accepted them, impatiently. He caught the dead bird by the wing, walked over to the ditch and dropped it.

'Say a prayer we won't have any more trouble,' said Mam.

Ann hugged herself with glee, she'd be too late to attend the ceremony now. He drove slowly the rest of the way to town, straining his neck to see the road clearly. He dropped them off at the side entrance. The church was crowded, with people standing three deep in the aisles. Ann was squashed into a seat beside two old men. The priest stood, hands outstretched at the offertory. The middle of the church was divided into black and white, boys and girls. Girls began to float to the altar, like dandelion puffs, and walked back, right past the block where Ann sat. She bent down further behind the man in front, and kept her hands over her face. Mary Sherlock was the first to appear, her eyes round and solemn, her hands joined under her nose. Sr Ignatius stood near the altar, directing the traffic. Dad motioned her to move. The hymn being sung by the choir seemed to gather momentum as the sound swept forward.

'Ga-ther round,
the table of the Lord,
eat his bod-y,
drink his blood,
and we'll sing a song of Love.'

She walked to the altar behind the last of the stragglers. As she got nearer, her legs trembled, blood thudded in her ears. She kept her eyes glued to her joined hands as she crossed to kneel. The sway and tremble of the altar boy's smock came closer and closer. A salver was placed under her mouth. She held out her tongue and felt a disc as light as a feather laid there. As she turned to walk back, she caught the full horrified stare of Sr Ignatius. The thought of swallowing the feather almost made her retch. She hurried back to her seat, almost running. Placing the white handkerchief Mam had given her in her hands, she knelt, and spat the host into it.

'Mass is ended, go in peace.'

At once, people clogged the narrow doors. Someone jabbed her shoulder sharply,

'I want to talk to you Miss.'

Dad smiled and nodded encouragingly to her. Ann followed the nun, up the empty centre of the church, past the altar and into the sacristy.

'Now I want to know what is the meaning of this?' Sr Ignatius said pointing to the dress. Ann stared at her hands.

'Did you not give that note to your mother? How dare you attempt to receive a sacrament in that thing and look at me when I'm speaking to you. This isn't the last you'll hear of this. Oh I've seen many straps like you in my day and I know who you model yourselves on, not our Blessed Mother Mary, oh no, on Mary Magdalene, a fancy woman, making your first communion in blue!'

Ann heard herself say,

'It's not blue, it's turquoise.'

The nun watched her, her face as stiff as cardboard.

'Get out, get out of my sight.'

Ann shot out the side door and ran around the front. Mam and Dad stood in a huddle with other parents near the gates. While he was talking to Mr Sherlock, Dad placed his hand on her head, pressing the crown of flowers into her scalp, his other hand held her bag and gloves. As they walked to the car, Mam asked,

'Well, how did you like it?'

'Sr Ignatius said I was like Mary Magdalene in this dress,' Ann said.

'Did she now?' said Mam, smiling, amused by this. 'You look very nice in it, all the same, turquoise suits you.'

Tricia stood at the car, smirking, then she hissed,

'You've got to get your photo taken yet, and you've got to go around and visit people.'

Mam sat in the front dabbing perfume behind her ears. As Dad started the car, she said,

'You know Sean, this town may have possibilities after all.'

'Is that so?' he said, turning down the main street.

Jack Gannon, stood at Gorry's newsagents with his

cronies. A dog trailed in front of the car, its tail swinging widely.

'Where to first?' he asked.

'I think we'll celebrate,' said Mam. 'Go to McGinn's Hotel.'

Ann kicked at the seat in front of her, scuffing her new, black patent shoes,

'I'm going to have it out with you tonight God, you and me are finished,' she promised.

Sheba Feminist Publishers also publishes other books for children, younger readers and adults too. We are happy to send you a free catalogue and any books you would like to order right to your door! Please add 75p p&p for each book you order.

The Playbook For Kids About Sex
Words by Joanie Blank
Pictures by Marcia Quackenbush
Now in its second edition, this excellent workbook, illustrated with simple line drawings, encourages the reader to play an active role in open discussion about sex. Age group 8 - 11 years.
£3.99 ISBN 0 907179 16 9

Changing Images: Anti-Racist, Anti-Sexist Drawings
Drawings by Natalie Ninvalle
Introduction by Kate Myers
New ways of seeing are explored in this collection intended specifically for use in schools and community centres. A much needed portrayal of how our society actually looks — lively and realistic images which replace the bland stereotypes we see everywhere.
£2.00 ISBN 0 907179 24 X

Aditi and the One Eyed Monkey
Suniti Namjoshi
A modern and witty fairy tale in which an elephant, an ant, a monkey and an Indian princess team up for a quest for the beautiful and wayward dragon who holds their land hostage. The nonviolent solution to their problem makes wonderful sense. A fairy tale that subtly questions the values of the traditional, and creates magic anew.
£2.95 ISBN 0 907179 30 4